SELECTED STORIES

Benny Andersen

Selected
Stories

Curbstone Press

These stories are selected from *Puderne* and
Tykke-Olsen m. fl., both published by Borgen
Forlag, Copenhagen, Denmark.

this book has been published
with the support of:

The Connecticut Commission on the Arts
The Danish Ministry of Culture
The Augustinus Foundation

Danish ISBN: 87-418-5478-0

U.S. ISBN: 0-915306-25-5

LC: 82-23459

distributed in Denmark by:
BORGEN FORLAG

published by:
CURBSTONE PRESS
321 Jackson Street
Willimantic, CT 06226

Selected Stories

CONTENTS

Introduction

When Danish post-war literature during the 1950's broke the constraints of its first phase of Modernism, one that had been characterized by an intense fascination on the part of Danish poets with European Symbolism, Benny Andersen, born in 1929, was among those young authors who began to develop a distinct style of their own. He and other poets would no longer follow the artistic ideals of the literary camp around the prominent journal *Heretica* (1945-1953) which had come increasingly under attack for having fostered an obscure symbolic language. Andersen's debut as a lyric poet, while closely linked with the *Heretica*-group, can be considered to have taken place a second time at the beginning of the 1960's with a collection of poems that clearly indicated his departure from this Danish Modernism that was developed mainly during the 1940's. Instead, an authentic literary voice expressing Andersen's existential concerns began to emerge and was carried over into the other genres with which he worked in subsequent years, be they dramatic works, children's books, the short story or the novel. In line with his demand in one of his earlier poems, to "spit out/ even if stains should get on existence," he proceeded by bidding farewell to the false paradise of a modern consumer-oriented society. Following the horrors of World War II and the onset of the Cold War, he exposed the mechanisms commonly used for building up an illusion of security in the face of a deeply felt threat to human existence and to non-materialistic values. With his extensive variations of the fundamental theme of the difficulties surrounding a genuine balance in life for the individual, Andersen has become a literary moralist in the Scandinavian tradition of Kierkegaard, Ibsen, and Strindberg, and, moreover, he can be placed in the European tradition following Dostoevsky, Kafka, the French Existentialists, and the Theater of the Absurd. Combining a humanistic ethos with the conviction that the ridiculous must be taken seriously, he explores human fears and insecurity as they range from the demonic to the grotesque.

While focusing on the individual in everyday life, Andersen scrutinizes our social norms and the standard of life we have created in our Western industrialized society, and he questions critically the quality of life we uphold and export. Andersen's social criticism does not, however, merely expose the ills of a modern utilitarian society, but centers primarily on the individual's adaptation to values and roles within that society. He takes issue with the short-cuts taken by those who fail to choose genuine personal development and therefore must face the lack of authentic balance in life. Andersen's dialectical pattern of thought underlying the depiction of such a difficult pursuit of balance is explicit in the tragicomic figure of the first-person narrator in most of his stories. Here he formulates predominantly the conflicts encountered by the individual who either does not perceive or shirks the responsibility of personal development and compensates for this neglect by adapting to superficial behavioral norms. Those norms, supplied and promoted by society, falsely insure social acceptance and success. But neither the choice of pursuing a mere social identity nor the passive resistance to society as an outsider are depicted as acceptable solutions. Personal development in accord with a humanistic stance can be sensed as Andersen's ethical imperative, a key factor for improving the quality of everyday life and, at the same time, an individual potential that needs to be activated. As in this volume's selection from Andersen's two collections *The Pillows* and *Fats Olsen and Other Stories*, it is from the perspective of the so-called average person that

Andersen presents a spectrum of his basic concerns; in particular, he uses a close-up technique for creating awareness of the seemingly trivial, yet often detrimental patterns of conduct in human relationships.

In a most persuasive manner, Andersen's first-person narrators present their cases, frequently to anonymous listeners; they subtly target the reader for an individualistic perspective that justivies all their behavioral quirks. The protagonists usually couch their present conflicts in past experiences by reflecting upon and analyzing these experiences in retrospect, as well as by using an apparently digressive mode of narrative that meanders between the past and the present, and main and secondary actions. While relating the crisis they feel, or feel compelled to explain, the narrators at the same time reveal their social environment—the major characteristics of which are enervating everyday battles, small everyday brutalities, and coldness and aggression among people, all of which generate feelings of individual helplessness, of isolation, and often of despair, feelings that must be responded to for the sake of individual survival. Usually, however, the response comes in the form of a short-term solution which grants but short-range relief. Andersen magnifies this thematic seriousness by means of uncommon focus and close observation, including self-observation on the part of the narrator-protagonist. He thereby exposes intolerance toward others, which is acted out privately or publicly if not directed against the self, pointing to the daily more or less subtle acts of violence people commit against each other and themselves. Tendencies toward Fascism in everyday life become visible, with the individual emerging as creator of his or her own misery and as contributor to common obstacles for meaningful self-development and interaction with others.

It was not until recently that Andersen turned more directly to his reader with a practical application of his ethical convictions to daily life. This can be seen in "The Speaking Strike", a key chapter from his first novel *On the Bridge*, published in 1981. Focusing on the sphere of the developing adolescent against the background of Greater Copenhagen during the occupation by Nazi armed forces in 1944, Andersen delineates the intense search for a valid stance toward others in his portrayal of the fourteen-year-old Erling Larsen and his alter ego Allan Nielsen before their graduation from school. Besides the close resemblance to the more expansive genre of the *Bildungsroman*, this thematic nucleus is given an added historical dimension through the war events of 1944 because, parallel to the contrastive individual self-assertion of Erling and Allan, we also witness the self-assertion of the Danes through their increasingly open resistance to the occupation forces of Nazi-Germany. "The Speaking-Strike" depicts Andersen's ethical pursuit and the challenge he voices to any one-sided perspective through his dialectical interplay of the serious and the humorous dimensions of a critical situation, here perceived with the sensitivity of the adolescent's point of view. Similar to the French Existentialists, Andersen places specific emphasis on the responsible choices each individual must make in order to develop and contribute to a more authentic life, starting in the unidealized everyday sphere. He thereby indicates his commitment as an author to being actively involved in shaping the values of contemporary society, and thus he is essentially in line with the demands affecting the artist's role in society, as it was heatedly debated among Danish intellectuals during the post-war period.

The following selection of stories is aimed at acquainting the English-speaking readers with a representative cross-section of Andersen's narrative works to date. It intends to provide an impression of the scope of his work, besides complementing the anthology of his *Selected Poems* already available in English translation. When considering Andersen's popularity in Denmark as well as abroad—his poems and stories have been appearing in the major European languages—it can be said that Andersen promises to transcend national boundaries to become another well-received ambassador of Danish literature who, not unlike Hans Christian Andersen, runs the risk of a one-sided reception, in his case that of being regarded as merely a clever humorist. For this reason, the anthology of stories presented here pays special attention to one of Benny Andersen's techniques that poses the greatest difficulty for rendering his works into any language; his linguistic experimentation, that is, the often humorous and thematically crucial play upon Danish idioms. As much as possible, the translations in this edition have preserved the ambiguity and the elegance of Andersen's word play in order to reduce the possibility of misunderstanding him as a mere humorist.

For the reader who wishes to obtain a survey of the literary tradition in Denmark and of the modern developments in the main genres, the short annotated bibliography at the end of this volume may serve as a guide to sources from which a context for Andersen's works can be established. References to additional English translations of Andersen's stories and to works of literary criticism that are available in English are also supplied in this list.

The Pants

Okay, okay, I'll get to the point. I'm in the tiny minority, and so I've got to get to the point. The majority never needs to explain itself, it's explanation enough that they are the majority. Not so many details, you say, but it's not so easy to say off the cuff what's important and what's not. Take the dairyman I trade with, for example, he has a glass eye. So what, you ask; and yet I recently bought half a pound of butter, and when I went to butter bread for my lunch the lump of butter suddenly gave me a stony stare. Now he has got a larger size of eye, but I was so shocked that I changed to margarine and in that way I got back my childhood taste for margarine on rye bread. So much welled up in me, and I think that made me buy those pants.

You see, as a child I got a bum deal on clothes, I got my brother's old rubber boots, sweaters, lumpy mended socks, coats, books, toys, I made an awful commotion every time, but there were no two ways about it, I had to be a good boy and accept my place in line. But now that I'm alone and getting on in years and can buy my own clothes, I go and rummage in boxes of used clothing, I feel naked in a tailor-made suit. At the second-hand clothing store and at auctions I buy shoes and clothes that have belonged to other people, watches, suspenders, pants, hats, it's a relief to slide into a pair of pants that have been walked in, sat in, and sometimes pissed in, too. A calm comes over me. All my worries fall into the cuffs, ready to pour out every now and then along with the gravel and chaff which usually collects there. Yes, I've noticed that cuffs are out now. Why don't they knock down the street curbs, too, and let the dirt blow around freely? With cuffs you're sure where

1

the dirt is.

With this taste of margarine in my mouth I knew I had to get myself a pair of secondhand pants, I needed to refresh that feeling again. So yesterday I found a pair in a little shop I usually go to. They were dark brown, the seat was beginning to droop, there were a couple of bulges at the knees as if they'd been worn by a horse, but I don't care too much if they fit or look nice. What matters is that they have personality, that they have atmosphere. Of course they had been cleaned after the previous occupant, but I could taste their special scent of something melancholy and faithful, which really appealed to me and at the same time made me excited, I could hardly keep myself from putting them on before I got home. Let me tell you, every time I put on old rags like this, their atmosphere seeps into me and makes me behave differently than I usually do, they draw me towards parts of town where I've never been before, make me talk to total strangers the clothes may know.

These pants drove me down towards the harbor, but not the part I usually go to, they led me out of the main street, the fancy shops disappeared and little bars showed up, but the pants continued on to the last one. You couldn't see what it was like in there, the curtains were drawn, so from the outside it looked really dreary and boring, and who feels like going in there? But I couldn't do a thing, that was the place the pants had decided on.

It wasn't so bad in there, even though there wasn't exactly linen on the tables, there was green linoleum where the dice could really tap dance. Nice people, a little loudmouthed but not really drunk, coats on and caps on the table, so they had to move them every time the dice were about to roll into them, so better on the floor, obviously there was a terrific back and forth of caps and bottles. I kept my coat on and asked for a beer and a bottle of stout. I was really satisfied with the pants. At first I felt a little uneasy, but now I patted them and enjoyed

2

sitting down without their getting tight around the knees like new ones.

There was a lady sitting by herself in a corner, a pretty woman, in her thirties I would guess, dark coat and fur hat, a sort of Russian style hat, a little full in the face, eyes nearly stout-brown, her mouth looked as if it wanted to cry, but actually I wasn't sitting watching her, I'm finished with that chapter. The last girl I had was named Ruth, and one day as we were lying on the sofa doing it she said just what I needed: your ceiling needs painting, Karl. So it came to a stop all by itself, because it wasn't Ruth or anyone else I was interested in, it was a small frightened girl long ago, it had something to do with wet trees and benches, little hands in big pockets and big hands in little ones and a treat of rum balls and chocolate mints, that was what I couldn't forget, everything else was just cotton and bandages. Of course I kicked Ruth out, but I ought to be damned grateful to her for that line, it could not have been said more plainly. After that time I began to buy my beer at different places, my consumption increased, you know, and I don't like to be conspicuous. Stout and schnapps, alcohol to clean the greasy thoughts with. Okay, I'll get to the point, but all of this is part of what happened. You should damned well be more nervous that I'm forgetting something, because *I* am. Let me see now, about that lady, it was something with the pants, either they caught sight of her or she caught sight of them. She looked over at me, but I think she looked at the pants, too, and then she got nervous, began to dig in her purse for lipstick, put it down again, looked around for the waiter but then looked over at me again, or at the pants, when he caught her glance. I can only see one explanation for her nervousness: there was something between her and those pants, maybe she had been expecting the pants but not with me in them. And then a remarkable thing—here you must promise not to interrupt me—the pants began to get tight around the knees, they made me stand up and walk over to her. Yes, maybe you don't see anything strange in that, you think to yourself: what an old tom cat. But that's because you haven't paid attention to the details, they're what's important. The pants wanted to go over to her, and for reasons of modesty I had to go along. So there I sat. And the pants couldn't talk, I had to speak up for them, and at first I sat there and tried to figure out what they wanted.

Well, of course at first I said, what would you like to drink? Idiotic: she was sitting there with a glass of liqueur.

"Thanks, I have one," she said. Look, it's here I think we have a clue. Otherwise she might have said: will you leave me alone, just what do you take me for? Or this: thanks, honey, what can you afford? But she said what I said, and I think that must be proof she knew those pants pretty well. As soon as I had sat down, she put her hands up on the table and rested them there. I thought: now we've got to figure this out, take it easy—if those pants want something it will be clear. And so I sat as quiet as a mouse and felt it penetrate me. Something was wrong somewhere. Someone had been hurt, maybe her, or him in the pants, or both of them. A clamminess came from the pants that sent goose pimples up my thighs.

I stared at her hands lying right across from mine. Her fingertips lightly touched the green tabletop. My own carrots were lying in the same way, and my square, yellow, cracked fingernails stared right at hers, which were elegant, translucent like the petals of a flower you hold up to the light. Then she turned her fingers in under her palms, and at that my fingers really went crazy, they reached across toward hers, crept over the table and reached under hers in order to open them again, but it was still the pants that were behind all this, and she didn't move her hands, she didn't open them either, but let my fingers stay there halfway under hers, and it was only then I looked up. Her eyes were round and black now, I thought at first it was me she was looking at, but it was something right behind me.

"What's going on here?" a shrill jagged voice like a boy's who is trying to make his voice sound grownup, so I was a little flabbergasted to see a gigantic man step up to the table. I drew my fists back. Her hands jumped into her purse and hid.

"Not a thing, it was just . . ." She tried to smile, I guess she wanted to say: it was just the pants, but that wouldn't have been understood in the right spirit. I kept my trap shut, I didn't get any orders from the pants.

I disliked his face instantly, but that, too, has to be understood in the right spirit, because I have friends who look at least just as unpleasant without it bothering me, the same small, distrustful foxy eyes in a big puffy mug, the same broad, self-righteous mouth, I've never been able to understand what pleasure women can get from a face like that, but they were good buddies, and I think he and I could have had many good drinks together, too, if we had met each other and I hadn't had those pants on.

"Did he bother you?"

"No, not at all, we were having a chat, it's nothing at all."

A chat. We'd hardly said a word. Honestly, I was moved by the way she covered for me, even though it was the pants she was worried about, but at the same time she said it was nothing at all. I was moved and relieved and at the same time damned mad at the way women humiliate themselves for men and are afraid of them because they are big, self-confident and jealous. I got up. He moved in front of me.

"Do you have to go now, just when I've arrived, that's kind of strange," he said sweetly.

It helped a little to stand up, even if he was still a head taller than me. But in the course of time I've learned that the worst thing you can do when you're next to tall people is to lay your head back and address their nostrils, they really enjoy that and hold their noses just so, inhale blissfully and clap you on the shoulder as if they were forgiving you some old debt. I stared right at the knot of his tie, which was very full and neat as opposed to mine, which looks like a tied-off intestine, and said:

"Yes, now that you mention it, it is rather strange. I'll go and think it over a little."

Then he stepped aside. The crap shooters had become quiet, I heard only her trying to straighten things out.

"I'm telling you, he was so polite . . ."

"Yes, anyway he shook your hand, I saw."

I waded out into the cold. It was windy, the pants flapped around me. I hurried away from the place.

Now fall had come. When I had tramped out there I didn't give it much thought, I was more anxious to know where we were going, me and the pants. But now I saw it. Haven't you ever noticed that it can be fall for a long time before you actually realize it. Of course, you know it, for sure, and if someone asked: what season is it now? you would answer right away: fall, of course. But suddenly one day you see it, the leaves lying trampled on the wet flagstones, the wind up the pantlegs, you feel some strange sinking motions in your heart, ugh, it's fall now, and you are surprised that it first strikes you now, even though you've been aware of it for several weeks, but in such an absent-minded way, but now you're caught up in it yourself and can't get out of it just like that even if you wanted to. You are yourself one of the greasy leaves being trampled awry, there isn't a damned thing you can do about it. By the way, it's something the same with spring now that I think about it—ok, ok, fine, we'll stick to fall. As I said I was walking along staring at the fallen leaves, I must have been really feeling low because I don't remember anything but cobblestones and paving, cigarette butts, dog turds, tin foil, there was an incredible amount of tin foil, the kind that candy bars, chocolate mints and that sort of thing are wrapped in, that's about the saddest thing you can see, that kind of discarded, crumpled tin foil that's been walked on by wet shoes. I was walking along there and was really unhappy about that story, but I thought to myself, it won't do a damned bit of good, you should just keep out of it, those two will figure it out, forget it, it's not like you to take it so hard, think of your own troubles, maybe that will cheer you up a little. And that's what I did, yes, indeed it was easy enough, all too easy, I went and slipped on the dead tin foil. She was really afraid of me, the kid was. I didn't want to hurt her, but the only thing that would calm her down was chocolate mints, I stuffed her with chocolate mints, but there weren't enough chocolate mints in the country to quiet her down, the poor kid. Seventeen, I think she was, and I was in my early twenties. I had had several, but never in that way, there was none of that sort of thing, I wanted to make her happy, she was like a little sister, I've only had brothers, a sister to take good care of, give some nice clothes to, be kind and polite to, take along to some of the good movies, get to smile now and then—now don't interrupt me, or else I'd rather just shut up.

Well, it didn't work out. And the worst of it is that I saw her later. It was enough to drive you to drink, if you didn't already. I myself had gone out looking for a pickup, on my way into one of those places with red neon lights over the door and a people-wise, unfriendly doorkeeper right inside the door, and I step aside for a couple coming out, a fat guy with a girl, it was her, thank God she didn't see me. She was laughing loudly about something or other, but I could have done without that laughter. It wasn't a matter of chocolate mints anymore, it wasn't a matter of anything. There simply aren't enough chocolate mints in the world.

Yes, so there I was walking along brooding with my hands in my pockets and my chin between my lapels. I didn't see where I was going until I suddenly stopped at the edge of the pier. There was a strong wind, the water sprayed up toward me. It was cold to stand so far out, but still I stayed there, I don't know, the whole thing was strange. Your ceiling needs painting. And what then, once it's been painted?

7

Actually I had gotten pretty far out along the pier. Nobody lived here, just locked warehouses and naked cranes the wind was whistling through. A single, unlighted coal barge lay creaking in its moorings, otherwise all the boats were snug and secure farther inside the harbor, and there were lights and people and bars in there too. By now the two of them had gotten home and they were fighting about me, or about him who was the first to wear the pants. Maybe he beat her up, he actually looked the type, the big bully, because he didn't get ahold of me. And she probably bawled and cringed, warded him off with her fur hat and purse. But at the same time maybe she thought she deserved it because of what she had done to the other guy, hurt him so he left and stayed away for several days. That had surely happened over and over and he had returned every time, but women want to see how far they can go, it's as if they want to figure out something that way, how pretty they are, how impossible to do without. But in the end she figured it wrong after all, went a bit too far, and then he came out here just like me, and then, I guess, he jumped into the drink.

But that was all that stuff I didn't want to think about anymore, and I didn't want to rack my brain about my own fate, either, how was I going to entertain myself then, think ahead—of new margarine sandwiches, of new drinking buddies who are so well supplied with their own miseries that you don't feel like mentioning your own—there also might be something at the movies worth seeing, but I've stopped that too. I can't concentrate anymore on what goes on on the screen. What's happening is down in the theater. There are so many people around me who have each other to sit by, a big hand and a small hand meet in a bag of licorice drops so it rips and the drops spill down under the seats like dice, the chocolate mint is broken in half and like a gentlemen he gives her all the tin foil—no, I don't get much out of the movie and way too much out of the rest, so I'd rather have some colored bottles at home, sit and stare at the ceiling. It needs to be painted. And what happens when it's painted. And why were you afraid of me, you poor little thing, I just wanted the best for you. Oh, shut up, one should stop thinking for good.

There was a sort of landing place right down at the water's edge, like a drawer that's pulled out. I walked down the stone steps and tried to stop thinking. The water was sloshing up. I shuffled back and forth and was about to go up again but suddenly one of my shoes took a good gulp, it really went in, what the hell, it had been a while since I'd washed my feet, so I stood still and let the water splash around my shoelaces. Just stop trying to figure things out. After all, you have stopped so much, why not stop that too, why not stop completely—be free, get off—cross your heart, is there anyone who would miss you? I stood and froze with my hands in my pockets, my lighter was in there, out with it. There wasn't even a splash, at least not one that differed from the other splashes and noises. One splash among the others. Just a foretaste. My pipe was in the left pocket, out with it, now you've stopped smoking at the same time. Then off with your coat. It lay on top of the water for a while and tried to calm the waves a little with sleeves spread out, to comfort them a bit. One of the tails sank, still it stayed afloat, there was probably a little air left in the pockets. That irritated me. My shoes were wet anyway. I couldn't get the laces untied, so I tore them loose. One went too far out, the other one landed in the middle of the coat, then it finally began to sink. Now I was really freezing, but that didn't matter, that was also one of the things I wanted to stop doing. I bent my knees and stretched out my arms, but that was too much like the starting position at swimming meets, and in this case it was a matter of not swimming. It was probably better to just step over the edge and let oneself sink. Then it occured to me that I've always hated getting water in my ears. I rooted around in my jacket pockets, there was everything else there but cotton. However, my tobacco was in the inside pocket, so I stuck a good plug into each ear.

9

Now I should be ready. But which leg should go first? I tried to remember which leg I usually start with, but that's one of those things you never seriously try to get firmly established, and then when it really counts, you're left standing there. In that situation you simply lack know-how. I could also take off sideways, or backwards, or I could lie down and roll off the edge. The longer I remained standing, the more confused I got because of the many possibilities. The pantlegs by now were sopping wet at the bottom and were plastered around my shins, the pants really ought to be able to give me a clue, it was they that had started all this. I stared down at them, and then my knees began to shake, but now it wasn't because of the cold. It was the pants that wanted to come down here, it was them who wanted me to do kneebends at the water's edge, because it's dead certain that I've never claimed that existence was magnificent, on the contrary, life is troublesome, but still it has certain advantages, such as stout, nope it was those damned pants that had the terrible itch to get down to the drowned candidate. He might have had a pair of new, blameless pants on that day and left the old ones in the lurch, and now they wanted to go down to him, but that had to be without me. Quick as a flash I got them off and threw them out. First one leg sank and fluttered back and forth under the water as if it was looking for something, then the other one joined it, and then they agreed completely, that was exactly the direction they had to go, and in half a second they pulled the sagging bottom and everything with them. I raised the jacket collar up around my ears, hurried up the steps and homeward.

I understand very well that you did a doubletake when you saw me at full gallop heading down the street in my jacket, underwear and wet socks, but this is the pure, absolute truth, and the reason I didn't stop the first time you shouted was probably because of the tobacco in my ears, I almost couldn't get it out again. And I don't mind, either, staying overnight here at the station tonight, chief, I realize it won't do any

10

good to claim that I am more sober than I've been for a long time—and if to top it off you would loan me a pair of pants to wear home tomorrow morning. But you've got to promise me one thing: I'd like to know a little about the pants first, whether they belonged to a rummy, a pimp, or maybe a male prostitute. You can certainly understand that I've become more particular after this experience.

Hiccups

As far back as I can remember, I've enjoyed hiccuping, and my only regret is that I cannot bring the hiccups on in the way one evokes other pleasurable sensations. They choose their own day and time. To be sure, they can arise in connection with rapid consumption of cold liquids, but then don't think that I can get them going by swilling cold water or beer. That usually only causes a sick stomach; hiccups can't be forced.

But when the miracle finally happens, I have to watch out. First of all I must be careful not to attract attention, and since hiccups almost always turn up when I'm at a party with many people, the situation is difficult, especially since the highest degree of enjoyment is to emit a real loud, uninhibited hiccup. So I try to hold it in first gear, and for the time being it just thumps a bit in my throat now and then or manifests itself through a sudden jerk of the head which can be camouflaged with ordinary nods or by tossing my hair back as if a fly were bothering me. Afterwards I may discreetly look around for a way out so that I can smuggle my hiccup out into the hall, into the garden or to the bathroom where it can finally sing out, but alas, only seldom do I get that far, for as a rule some sharp ear or eye has observed me: "Oh, you have the hiccups—I can cure that."

The cold water with which one usually starts the treatment isn't that bad. In the beginning I was nervous about it, but now I know that the hiccups aren't damaged by it, just as little as by vinegar with sugar in it and whatever else one comes up with as the unfailing remedy. I calmly drink these things, joylessly, in order to show my good intentions. For I'd just as well not say that I should like to keep my hiccups; people think that I want to avoid imposing on them and find me only the more touching and helpless: "That is really admirable of you to pretend that it doesn't bother you, but we'll help you, just rely on us."

Now comes the hard test; I stand on my head; I stand on one leg with a glass of water on my forehead; but I submit to everything in order to keep a good relationship with the other guests, and I do want to be invited again, not because the party interests me especially but because being together with many festively clad people puts me into that vibrant mood which constitutes such fertile ground for my hiccups.

Next I count backwards from fifty with my mouth full of water, and blushing I dry the drops of water off my jacket when, at twenty-four, a powerful hiccup blasts the water out of my mouth. But people smile encouragingly; the fact that I am a difficult case only increases the suspense. It would indeed be sad if the hiccups had capitulated already because of a sip of water; no, this is better than any party game. The gentlemen take off their jackets and heatedly debate what one now should resort to; the ladies rush in and out with pitchers full of splashing cold water; after a while the floor is a mess.

But at a certain moment it becomes quiet, everyone is looking at me silently with sparkling eyes. I move up against the wall and lose a hiccup for it is clear to me that they are going to scare me. That has, to be sure, never damaged my hiccups, and I really have nothing against people suddenly shouting "Boo" behind me, if only I don't know it beforehand. But the fact that I know it makes me nervous. From what direction will it come, what can they come up with, who is going to start? Frightened, I stare at them; indeed, I'll give a start in acknowledgement if they will only hurry up and get it over with.

But now they can see I am on my guard. There is a continued silence; to be heard are only my recurrent hiccups which I now let have free rein, at least to enjoy them to the fullest as long as I may. But I can see the worst is on its way. They all know there is one remedy which never fails, and one they have kept 'til the end, after everything else was unsuccessful. They look at each other—who wants to take the initiative? There is no risk connected with it; the money is safe enough. Finally someone takes out his wallet, pulls out a ten-crown note and holds it up: One more hiccup, and it's yours. This is terrible. I try with all my might to hold the next hiccup down, in order not to offend anyone and not rob the man of this ten crowns which he does not dream of being in danger. I know it only makes things worse to hold back the hiccup, but what can I do aside from gaining time and hoping for a miracle—that suddenly the doorbell will ring or a thunderstorm will break loose or there will happen something entirely different which can distract their attention. I press my tongue back into my throat like a cork with the result that the hiccup, when it finally comes, takes a running start all the way down from my kidneys and blasts itself away out into the open with unbelievable power, so that I bang my head against the wall.

Everyone looks down into his coffee cup without moving or saying anything. For a moment the challenger stands paralyzed with his ten-crown note before flinging it over to me with a contemptuous air. And I am forced to take it. It isn't even of any use to say I am sorry; there is nothing to do. Everybody ignores me from now on. I can only wait for an opportunity to sneak out the door, downstairs and away, hiccuping sorrowfully.

After such an experience I keep to myself for a long time, but sooner or later my craving, not for company, but to hiccup, becomes so urgent that I again start to seek association with others and to ingratiate myself into social circles; now the question is to find some people who don't know me and my unfortunate inclination.

It is difficult in a smaller town constantly to re-establish a circle of acquaintances, I therefore have plans to move to the capitol; there should be plenty of possibilities there.

A Happy Fellow

My circle of friends sees me as a happy fellow, a lucky dog. They slap me on the back: "You lucky son of a bitch, with that wife and those kids, your business is thriving, you've still got all your hair, and you can play the banjo as well—aren't you happy?"

Yes, I should be happy, but I'm not. My handicap is that I don't really enjoy my own company. Once, long ago, I set great store in myself; however, the relationship has cooled considerably in recent years. But if you don't go in for yourself 100 percent, how can you mean something to others? How, for example, can you love your wife without pretending? She says proudly to our guests: "My husband is always in a good mood, handles every situation with a smile!" And the children tell their friends in high school: "Our father isn't like your fathers, who always want to put a damper on your fun and preach about how well off you are compared to when *they* were children!"

Actually I'm a dull person, who doesn't at all like my wife getting one parking ticket after another. As her kissing her cousin, the middleweight boxer, on the mouth; but, afraid to show how petty and jealous I actually am, I smile broadly in both instances and say lovingly: "That's alright, honey, you've got to sow your wild oats!" Whereupon she blushes and kisses me, saying: "You're a unique human being, the finest man I know." And I let her believe that.

Deep down, I'm revolted by the free upbringing we're giving our children, and, time after time, I have the overwhelming urge to beat some decent behavior into them, but instead I say: "To me, what you're doing seems silly, but since you learn best from you own stupid

17

mistakes, I'll just close my eyes—only give me a hint in advance when I'm to close them." My words hide no deeper meaning, but the children are delighted by their broad-minded father, and, as a result, I admit—behave themselves in a more exemplary manner than many of their peers who've had old-fashioned, bourgeois upbringings. Pure calculation on my part, because I don't want to lose their assurances of how good and fair a father I am. I'm simply afraid they'll discover what I'm really like and turn away from me. I have happiness, but can't enjoy it. I am always on guard to prevent the slightest scrap of my innermost self from showing, I sit on pins and needles, walk on red-hot coals, sleep on a bed of nails.

Once in a while I have to take a vacation by myself. "To unwind," I explain. Actually, to blow off steam. Alone in the summer house, I try to release enough of the pressure pent up inside me so that for the rest of the year I'll be able to enjoy my undeserved happiness—the friendship of my friends, the love of my family, and the favor of my business connections. I try to be the man I truly am, without smiles, frills, and liberal cliches. If my wife or my friends saw me now, they would be appalled. My children would develop irreparable complexes.

I walk down to the booth by the harbor to buy a freshly-caught plaice.

"Here, sir, alive and kicking."

"Hm. Are those red spots real? They look almost too natural. Are you sure it isn't flounder you've tattooed with red ink? I'm just asking."

The fishmonger lowers the scales in his hand. The red color spreading across his face is certainly real enough, but I stand my ground.

"Alive and kicking, you say. Hm. Frankly, I think it's been doped."

"It's been what?" he asks, half choking.

"Doped. It's been injected with a stimulant—or else you've put aspirin or hormones in the water."

Still the man manages to control himself; he turns stiffly to another customer.

"Hey," I say, "I'm not finished yet. See if you can't find a more likely plaice for me."

The fishmonger stands there bewildered for a moment, but then, deciding to regard me as someone mentally disturbed who must be humored, he comes up with another plaice.

"Have a look at this," he says with exaggerated friendliness, "not quite as big, but the small ones are best, you know."

I grab the flatfish with both hands and begin to rub its upper side.

"Hm. Yes, those spots look real enough."

He tears the fish away from me:

"Do you claim that . . ."

"I'm not claiming anything. I'm only saying that those spots *look* real enough. So for that matter, they might actually *be* real, right? My hands got sticky, can I just wipe them on your sleeve? Besides, I've changed my mind. I'd rather have a garfish. But the bones have to be genuinely green. I have it from a reliable source that fishmongers now and then have their assistants give the bones a once-over with verdigris—and I'll have none of that."

I manage to duck so that the plaice hits an elderly lady behind me instead. Unaccustomed to this sales technique, she falls over backwards into the eel tank. I take advantage of the general uproar to slip out and walk down to the dreary inn at the water's edge to eat—fried plaice.

The dining room is practically empty—usually, the guests first appear around eight, when the weather is tolerable; everyone has to go out on the jetty to catch a glimpse of the sunset after five days of continual rain. However there is one person sitting in the corner opposite me. Like me, he is eating plaice, poking at the fish with the same injured air as I, putting bones back on the tray with every indication of disgust, and suspiciously sniffing the remoulade. He

19

resembles me; I have an inner aversion to him.

The fish tastes excellent, so I decide the next time the rarely-sighted, nearly extinct waiter appears, I will tell him to advise the kitchen that the fish is overdone. I wipe my mouth and look up, catching sight of my fellow guest, who is wiping his mouth and looking up. We look at each other, both smile involuntarily, reach for our glasses to toast each other, both become shifty-eyed, drink without toasting, and continue to eat with short, hurried glances at one another as we wring the fishbones out from between our front teeth. It is him I need.

I walk around the lake toward home, quickly, so as not to lose sight of him. The mosquitos are annoying, but I don't stop to beat them off; on the contrary, I swing my right arm in the air until the veins stand out, then serve up the back of my hand for the beasts; a mosquito lands on it, finds secure footing, wipes its sticker, and buries it to the hilt. I'm about to smack it but then have a nastier idea; I tickle it a little so that, in fright, it tugs itself loose from its sticker and flies away, amputated from its vital organ. The back of my hand itches, but my heart glows. Promising evening.

The lake's two swans lie hunched up with their eight young between them—what are they called, swanlings? The man from the inn has disappeared at a turn of the shoreline close to the landing stage. I speed up and scout the path ahead. No one in sight. He may have hopped up onto a sidepath on the bank above the lake. I take a deep breath. I'll probably see him some other day. The rushes murmur slightly—maybe fish, maybe some ducks sleeping restlessly. A boat is moored there.

I'm about to turn around and continue homeward when, suddenly, a bell chimes, and my head is the bell that's chiming. I stand there looking at the stump of a thick branch in my hands and think confusedly: how did that get there? Shoved from behind, I tumble out onto the narrow landing stage, but regain my balance, turn around, and there before me stands the man from the inn. He has obviously smelled a rat, was lying in wait for me, and crowned me with a heavy branch. I'm still holding the heaviest end of the branch, which happened to fall into my hands when I reached out to steady myself. I begin to advance toward him to prevent his forcing me out onto the landing stage, but I check myself and voluntarily start to walk backwards along the plank while I feel the bump I've received on my head.

"What would you have done if I'd fallen into the water and was drowning?"

I wonder if I wouldn't have stood here to prevent you from making a final attempt to get out," he says smiling.

"I like that," I smile back. "My name is Christiansen."

I hold out my right hand, having previously shifted the club to my left.

"Pedersen, at your service," he answers and carefully puts two fingers toward my hand. The club doesn't crush his temple as intended, but strikes his shoulder, knocking him into the water.

When he breaks the surface with a gurgle, I ask attentively:

"Should I stand here to prevent you from making a final attempt to get out?"

Just as he is about to answer, he goes under, only producing a string of untranslatable bubbles illuminated by the sunset.

The club has fallen into the water. I look around for a pole I can use to pin him to the muddy bottom, but the only poles around are those holding the boards of the landing stage together.

There's a splash at the end of the stage. I bound over toward it as he heaves himself aboard the boat. I grab hold of the mooring rope.

He pulls out a pocketknife and cuts the rope, the boat glides away from the landing stage, but he grabs an oar and poles himself back in to it.

21

"Out here on the lake," he says, "there's no one on the shore now, too many mosquitos. No one will see if one of us drowns. No one will believe it. Things like that don't happen here."

I jump into the boat. He rows, I grab the other oar and row the other way, the boat spins in circles.

"Beautiful evening," he says and throws his oar overboard.

I do the same, the boat drifts slowly out onto the lake.

"Don't you think it's deep enough here?" he asks a little while later.

"We'll soon find out," I say, and poke both my thumbs in his eyes, but he treacherously whips one of his legs up under me and tips me overboard.

I stand up with duckweed all over my head.

"Not deep enough," I splutter. I give the boat a hefty shove out toward the middle of the lake and jump in without any hindrance from him.

"What now?" he asks once we're near the middle.

"I have a proposal," I answer. "The drain plug. Unfortunate accident."

"Excellent," he smiles. "Sharks would have made things more exciting, but an excellent solution. It's probably farther to shore than you think."

"I swim better than you think," I say and pull out the plug, which I hand to him. He looks at it for a moment, then at me—then he throws it into the water.

"Are there any next of kin to whom you would like me to bring a final greeting?" he asks.

The water soon reaches our knees. I take off my sweater and am about to take off my shoes. But he keeps his jacket on, so I put my sweater on again, and at that moment the boat disappears beneath us.

It's farther to shore than I thought. For a while we swim side by side, then he chooses a route which he believes is shorter. Had I been alone, I would have drowned. Only the thought that he would triumph over me the next day infuriates me enough to fight my way into the rushes. I crawl through them on all fours, barely able to keep my head above water.

I guess I was lying on the shore for about an hour. Wake up from the cold and vomit a mess of water and tadpoles. Look around. Nothing to be seen. Maybe he's drowned, maybe he reached shore and went home.

The following day I go home. It would be just too annoying to meet him in town again.

"Why are you home after only one day?" my wife asks.

"It was simply the best vacation I've ever had," I answer.

"You do look refreshed and happy," she blushes, "I'm almost afraid to show you my latest parking tickets."

"To tell you the truth, I've actually missed them," I answer, touched.

She gives me a squeeze: "You're so good."

"But things are worse with the children," she continues. "They took advantage of your absence. They were driven home yesterday, dead-drunk, the two of them."

I go right up to their room and give them each a beer.

"Best thing for the morning after," I explain.

"The world's greatest father," they say, feeble and happy. "Don't you ever get mad?"

I just smile at them. For the first time, I feel I've really deserved the happiness that surrounds me.

Layer Cake

And here's the living room. You'll see in a little while, if you stay that long, it's sunny in here from three o'clock and on through the rest of the afternoon—when there is sun, that is. No, there's no bathtub, but that's the sort of thing I don't think you'll miss when you haven't got it in the first place. The vegetable store is across the street, and over there is the delicatessen—his liver pâté isn't always up to par, but all he needs is to be told off once in a while. The bakery is at the next corner; I was a regular customer there for many years, but not any more, though you don't need to feel any obligation on that score. Their bread was excellent. On Sundays we liked to have cookies with our afternoon coffee and Dam, the baker, made them just right—you know slightly sticky inside. First we'd stand outside the bakery looking at what was in the window, and I'd ask: "How about some coffee-cake, Henry, wouldn't that be nice for once? Or almond sticks?" Sometimes, when we were feeling really crazy we might even say, "How about a big nasty napoleon?"—I hope I don't offend you, it wasn't meant that way of course. "Or a chocolate eclair?" But we were used to being thrifty from our early years together, so we ended up with cookies. Nevertheless, I've asked him—not once, but hundreds of times—if he wouldn't like to have a piece of layer cake. I certainly wouldn't have begrudged him that, he was so thin and hollow-cheeked that I was almost ashamed to be seen with him on the street. I always made sure that he wore at least two sweaters under his coat to make him look a bit more impressive, so a few calories would have become him. But, "No-o-o," he always said, "it's too rich for me." So, it's no wonder that I believed him and kept on

25

buying cookies, is it?

The years went by and he got thinner and thinner; I put up with it, padded him well with woolen sweaters and scarves when we went out. His head, I couldn't do much about, of course, but with his collar well pulled up under his chin and his hat down over his eyes, nobody noticed anything.

Things went neither better nor worse than that my sister on Amager had a big party one Saturday, and I did all the cooking, and they were so pleased and ate so well that when they got to the coffee and layer cakes hardly anyone could eat another bite, and I ended up getting some pieces of the cake to take home with me.

The next day was Sunday, and at three o'clock Henry started to put on his sweaters and coat as usual, and I say: "Where are you going?"

"Aren't we going over to the bakery?" he asks.

"Not today," I tell him, "we've still got some layer cake left over from yesterday, so just take off your coat again."

But when I set the cake down in front of him, he gets even more quiet than usual and just stares at it.

"What's wrong?" I ask.

"Nothing, except that I can't eat it."

Here I must add that it was a beautiful cake with very fine texture, several layers of different jam fillings and a thick layer of whipped cream on top and it was decorated with orange slices and bits of chocolate and colored candies.

"What kind of nonsense is that?" I said. "Here we haven't had layer cake for twenty-one years, and when I finally give you a piece, you can't eat it."

"I never liked layer cake," he says looking down.

"Well I never," I say to him. "Here I am offering you something really delicious, instead of those same old cookies, and then you tell me that you don't like it. Maybe you want *me* to eat it—me, with my figure;

you're the one who really needs it."

But he looked so guilty that I didn't suspect anything, so I just said, "Well, we'll try a little later then."

When it was time for coffee that evening I set out the layer cake again, and this time I took a piece for myself to sort of encourage him a little. Well, he did take a bite too, but sat for a long time turning it around and around in his mouth. "Come on, man, swallow," I said. He did, and then he put down his fork.

"What's wrong with you?" I asked. "Am I supposed to sit here alone eating this cake, which isn't even good for me."

"It's too rich for me," he said, "you know that."

Well now, I'd like to ask you, when a man who hasn't had a decent piece of layer cake in twenty-one years finally gets a piece, why can't he eat it? I think there can be only one answer: somehow he's had enough layer cake. Anyone else would dig right in, even if he knew it would just go to his waistline, but he—who was skinny as a skeleton—he pushed it away.

So the question was: Where would somebody be fed so much layer cake that he couldn't get a bite of it down at home? Who can afford to stuff so much of it into a man that he actually becomes nauseated by it—remember, layer cake isn't cheap these days. I can only see one explanation: a woman who works in the bakery. With a job like that, a woman can always figure out a way when she gets a crush on a man. And here for twenty-one years, Sunday after Sunday, he had insisted that he didn't want any layer cake, that it was too rich for him—and I'd fallen for it every time, gullible as I am.

But nevertheless, I wanted to give him a chance, since we'd stuck together for so long, after all there are things that create bonds— memories and so forth. So when he came home from work the next day I asked as usual: "Are you hungry?"

"You bet, what have you got to offer?"

"Fried flounder, good and fresh. But first you have to eat your cake from yesterday, otherwise it'll get stale."

He got a very strange look on his face.

"Yes, but if I don't like layer cake..." he said. But now I let him have a piece of my mind.

"Look here," I said, "I don't know where you go and eat your layer cake, and I couldn't care less how much cake you eat when you're not at home. But if that makes you think you can turn up your nose at *my* layer cake, you've got another think coming."

He didn't know what to do with himself, and asked me to explain what I meant.

"I don't think I need to go into details," I just said.

So he himself took the plate with his piece of cake, and carried it into the living room. When I went in after a little while, the plate was already empty. But I wasn't completely convinced, because when one has eaten layer cake, there are usually a few smears here and there on the plate, yet this plate was practically clean. I should really have gone back to the flounder again, but I stayed in the living room dusting a bit and so forth. I looked in the wastebasket, I checked the cupboards, and then I thought of looking inside the wood-burning stove, and sure enough, there it lay, a pretty sight, with the whipped cream downwards.

I went into the kitchen and got another piece of cake.

"Now you eat it, while I'm watching you," I said.

"And if I can't?"

"You can't, eh? But when you are with your bakery woman it's no problem—there you can stuff yourself so much that it's impossible to get another piece down, even if it's your very own wife who is offering it to you."

"Ba-bakery woman?" he stammered.

"Yes," I said, "*bakery woman*."

He wanted to say something, but his mouth just opened and closed a couple of times, then he picked up the fork again.

"There's no need to look like that," I said. "I haven't put poison in it—not yet."

Suddenly he began stuffing it into himself in huge heaps and as soon as he was finished he rushed out of the room and threw up.

Well, if that isn't proof, I don't know what would be. Just imagine. He had such an overdose of layer cake at that bitch's place that eating one more piece made him throw up. And as if that wasn't enough, he didn't want any flounder either. That must have been some orgies they had! And here I've been waiting on him and darning his socks and looking after his goldfish for twenty-one years and I just thought he was a little slow. And then, in the course of twenty-four hours, an abyss of deceit suddenly opens up.

From then on, not a day went by that I didn't buy layer cake and forced it into him.

I clearly remember the last day he was at home, when he said:

"As long as I've got to eat something I don't like, can't you buy napoleons instead? I don't care for them either, but I think I could keep them down better."

At that point I lost my patience:

"That's what you'd like, eh? First gorge yourself on layer cake outside, and then continue with napoleons here at home—no sir, I'll have no respect for you until the day you ask me yourself for your layer cake here, in your own home."

He sat for a long time staring straight ahead, took a bite now and then, and when he had eaten half of the piece, he left the room. I thought he was just going out to throw up as usual, but he didn't come back. The next day his sister sent me a message saying he had moved in with her. Of course, he still has to pay me something but even so, it still doesn't add up to enough so I can afford to stay in a big apartment alone. That's why I want to exchange apartments with you.

I've seen him a couple times since; it was something of a shock, he'd almost gotten fat. I don't think that was very nice of him. It's as though he was showing that he hadn't gotten any decent food during those twenty-one years, and I have his own word that he did: "You're a good cook, at least one has to admit that," he used to say. The food just didn't stick to his ribs. Not before he moved.

It won't be easy to give up this window here. Perhaps I should tell you what he looks like, and maybe you could write to me if he passes by once in a while. That way it wouldn't seem as though I'm completely out of the picture.

Besides, I'm not really sure I want to exchange apartments with you. Your apartment isn't very big; I don't know how I'll find room for the furniture. But, anyway, I've got your telephone number, so I'll let you know one of these days. But, as I said, I don't think—yes, of course, I won't keep you then; I need to pick up a few things myself before the stores close—I'll see you out.

Fats Olsen

I'll probably have to cut down that apple tree. It's really too bad—
it's such a nice tree, bears good fruit, too, Cox orange pippins, not too
large, concentrated savor and juicy through and through. But things
can't go on like this. Or else I'll have to move. Sell the tobacco shop,
give up my editorial work and move. Not on your life. It would just be
the same thing all over again in a new place. And abandon the paper?
Never. Who would edit it then? None of the nitwits around here want
to write anything but soccer betting slips. And who but me wants to
spend most of his leisure time working at an unpaid job? No, if I drop
out, it will just turn into an advertising sheet again. No, it will have to
be the apple tree that goes. Poor, unsuspecting apple tree.

People are really very nice out here, toward each other anyway. By
and large. Not toward me. There's an explanation for that. But they
respect me as editor. And as a shopkeeper. And they're glad they can
come round back on Saturday afternoon when they've forgotten to buy
beer and cigarettes. You bet your life. But they'll certainly be careful not
to send one of the children. There's an explanation for that, too.
There's an explanation for everything, my father used to say. I don't
know whether he was entirely right, but anyway many things can be
explained if you take the trouble to get to the bottom of the matter. If
you overcome your aversion to using the inside of your head once in a
while. That's the thing that is a little scarce in these parts. They'd
rather wash their cars and discuss soccer over the hedge. And that's all
right, too, but it is certainly nothing that noticeably expands their
horizons. They assume that their way of living is the only right way—

all the others are fools not to see it. Look, people of this kind are not only naive, they can be dangerous, too. Once they begin to suspect that someone or other is a little different, it just takes a tiny spark and the whole lynch mentality explodes. Sometimes I try to smuggle a little sensible talk into the old rag. I've written short editorials and essays on tolerance, on respect for those who think differently, on democracy's possibilities today, on small-town mentality—for that's the funny thing about it all—that on the whole these people view themselves as superior, enlightened citizens of the world and in reality they are as narrow-minded as the peasant in Holberg's day. Well, maybe that's a little too harsh. Actually, I can't stand generalizing in this way—it's just as narrow-minded. Besides, there are some exceptions. But when they come into the shop the day after I've had some little thing in the neighborhood paper (and to their credit it must be stressed that they are extremely interested in what is in their "own" newspaper—that of course can also be seen as a clear expression of small-town mentality—well, enough of that) then they're impressed that I've been able to stick so many words together. Actually any high school student could have written the article as well or better. I graduated from technical school. (On the whole, I believe in the coming generations. They will become the true world citizens. For them discrimination and many other prejudices are completely absurd, which is probably the most important generation gap today, but I'll certainly be on guard against writing that—I have to watch my step, and anyway, the young people don't read the paper.)

Now take little Nina's father, Thorkildsen, he said: "What you wrote about the lynch mentality still thriving in the best of health was very interesting. It was something to think about. I just don't understand how you can grasp all these things and formulate them so clearly."

I thought: Sure, sure, Thorkildsen. If you'd used some of your leisure time when you were young to go to night school, if once in a while you cared to open a book, then you could probably train yourself to put words and thoughts together on a piece of paper, and then you wouldn't, I'm sure, be so impressed by my scribbling, which consists mainly of quotations from the essays and works of more talented people.—But I'm clever enough not to think that kind of thing aloud. I just said: "Oh, I don't have anything else to do evenings and it amuses me to piece things like that together, and it's nice that there's someone who cares to read it and think about it—that's enough satisfaction for me."

"Yes, I guess so," Thorkildsen said and got a little shifty-eyed. I knew immediately what it was he was thinking. It's a dangerous life I lead out here. Sometimes I get soaked in sweat thinking about what might happen. I am certainly big and strong, not to mention fat, and despite my nearly sixty years I can still lift a case of beer without getting a crick in my back. Strong beer at that. But if it came down to it would I be able to hit anyone? I've never been good at fighting, not even when I was a sailor. But now suppose you were afraid to die, suppose there were alot of people surrounding you and you panicked . . .

Thorkildsen is also a husky fellow and noticeably younger than I.

"Six pilsner and five soda water," he said. I bent down to get them.

"You might make one of the beers an export beer," he said. "Tell me, the beers are cold, aren't they?"

"Well, there's cold and cold," I said. "I can get some up from the cellar."

This balancing act. Not being too servile to him—that would strengthen any suspicion. Not too distant either.

"But you don't think that this lynch mentality could be thought to break out in our country—after all, isn't it too alien to us?"

"Hopefully it is—but we don't have so many blacks either—as yet. And the Greenlanders are far enough away. But then there are other

33

forms of discrimiation that under unusual circumstances could provoke something that perhaps isn't so far from lynching. Do you have a 10 ore piece?"

"Yes, I think so. Are you thinking of anything in particular?"

"I've several things in mind, but it's better that I write about this in a little more detail in some future articles. Would you like a bag?"

"No thanks, I have my briefcase. I think it will be interesting to read your next articles."

Yes, yes, Thorkildsen, Nina's father, has read and understood my article. Made an impression on him. Very interesting. And a week later forgot every word of it. Ready to tear my head off. Words. Paper. But anyhow, I really enjoy tinkering with it.

There's an explanation for that. Or several explanations. The children are afraid of me. Thank God. Well, still, I like children. Some children more than others. That's certainly very normal. I'm big and fat and my face is perhaps a little repulsive? Snubsnout. Comes from a time when I didn't want to hit first. A guy thought that I had winked at his girl. I explained to him that I had a nervous tick in one eye, something that I'd had since I was a child. And it was really true. I have them to this day even though there's a longer time between them now. But of course he said: Yes, sure you have, come on outside with me. That was in a dive in Aalborg. I was a sailor then, cook, wanted to see something of the world. I offered him a beer. No thank you, he said, but you can get a basting from me. He was a head and a half shorter than me so I didn't want to hit him. He hopped up on his toes and gave me one in the snout. There, we're even, he said. I hadn't even seen the girl, have often speculated over what she looked like. But that's where my snubsnout comes from. Everything has its explanation; in any case a snubsnout does. But back to the children. They're afraid of me but crazy about my apples. I'd gladly give them all the apples they could cram down their throats, but I don't even dare think about what would

34

happen then. That also has its explanation. The thing is that I live alone. I prefer to live alone and take care of myself but am neither a hermit nor misogynist. I occupy myself just as much with the world around me as with myself—it is, I dare say, fifty-fifty. Both in the shop and through my newspaper work I satisfy my need to associate with others. My old mother is worried about me: Why don't you get married? Look, I've clipped out the best matrimonial advertisements for you. Or at least take a housekeeper. I can't answer her except to say that it doesn't interest me. I'd rather have things the way they are. Naturally that's hardly a satisfactory answer for an old woman who has only one elderly son and no grandchildren. I've tried to find an explanation, and I've found one, too, which I can use for the present, anyhow, even if I don't think it is completely right. But right or not, why shouldn't you be permitted to live in the way that suits you best, provided that you don't cause harm to others—apart from your old mother? When I got married, she used to dread becoming a grandmother, and now she's ashamed that she isn't a great-grandmother at least.

If I were married now, or had a housekeeper, the children and I would have a far more relaxed relationship with each other. But now I'm under suspicion. It's the kind of thing that appears in little watchful glances and meaningful shifts in facial expression between the parents, brief comments, ostensibly harmless, yes friendly, poisoned candy. The parents tell their children: Don't go into Fats Olsen's yard and don't ever go into the shop alone to buy licorice. And of course never go into the back of the shop with him should it come into his head. And the children respond: Why not, Mother, what does he do there? Then there follows an exchange of meaningful glances between the parents. How much should we say, the mother asks silently and adds with her eyebrows: Now you must take over. And the father, irritated, says: You just listen to what your mother says—what your mother says is right.

Of course, I can't guarantee that the words fall exactly this way, but

I can read from the reactions of the children and the parents that the meaning and procedure has been thus. I had proof of this in an episode with Nina's father recently when Nina had been snitching apples with the others out in my yard. We'll come to that later, but now a little further into this interesting sociological process. Look, when the children don't understand half what their parents say, they elaborate on the innuendoes, talk with other children about it, put the different innuendoes together and try to fantasize or guess their way to a solution to the mystery of Fats Olsen. What takes place in his back room? I can see it when they come into the shop (two by two) and buy ammonium salts or comic books. They nearly stretch their necks out of joint to get a sidelong look into my back room—shouldn't there maybe be a rack or gallows in there, a single child's corpse or just a sawed off leg? In order to satisfy and calm their curiosity, I've become accustomed to letting the door to the back room stand open so they can see that it's entirely peaceful, if a little messy; a plush covered stool and a simple wooden table, where I read my newspapers and write my stuff for the paper, a couple of coathooks with jackets and overalls, a picture of the entrance to New York harbor (from my seagoing days), a wastepaper basket, a beer opener hanging on the wall from a string, a pair of wooden shoes for garden work. But then they cannot see what is hidden in the corner behind the flung-open door,—they try to catch a glimpse through the crack, maybe that's where Fats Olsen keeps his terrible secret, a sack of carved-up infants. They are violently curious to see the whole back room but at the same time would be terrified if I suggested that they peek in. But even if they acquired the knowledge that the back room held neither bloody footprints nor sinister implements, what about the cellar? Or the shed in the back yard? Or the rooms above? Even if I invited all the children and adults of the district for a sightseeing tour through the house with the right to overturn everything, rip open pillows and couchcovers, dig all through the

36

garden (that would please me, by the way,—I haven't gotten enough digging done) even then, in spite of everything, there would be a remnant of suspicion remaining: Yes, all the same, maybe he does it out in the woods then.

Maybe now you can see where I am heading: no matter how strong or independent a person you are, you're marked by your milieu, by your immediate surroundings and conditions. But you can also make your mark on your surroundings by virtue of the way in which you choose to react. I have to be a little more gruff with the children than I care to because every attempt at friendliness on my part would awaken suspicion. At the same time, with regard to the parents, I have to feign a surly relationship with the children because that will make them feel safer than if I were friendly toward them. The situation forces me to be outwardly different than I am. That is, bluntly speaking, what the milieu has done to me. Now we come to how I make my mark on my surroundings or try to. Partly through my local literary activities, which I mentioned before, and which I will return to a little later. But first and foremost through my reactions, or more correctly, because my reactions are very deliberate. If I chose not to give a damn what others thought about me and talked with the children as I wished to and tried to win their trust, sooner or later I would encounter a situation which would be misunderstood and thereby work up a hostile feeling toward me. Which in extraordinary circumstances could take on the character of a lynch mentality. So: by being pleasant and natural, I'd bring about disgusting characteristics in my fellow human beings. But if I choose the wisest course, to put on an act, not show myself too friendly to the children nor too hostile to them, either, then I should have a chance to maintain a kind of armed neutrality with the neighbors. So: by being a little gruff and by dealing in double-dealing, I am keeping the dangerous powers of my fellow human beings in check. I have often thought of writing an article in the paper on this interesting problem. Naturally, I wouldn't dare let it take place in the local situation—I'd transfer it to Tonga or Greenland, but anyway try to smuggle in some thoughts in which I could get folks hereabouts to make certain comparisons.

But then something happened which—I won't say destroyed my theories, but in any case turned them topsy-turvy.

First was the episode with Nina and the apple. I'm worried that the youngsters now and then when I'm away, or when they think I'm away, will go apple stealing in my yard. It's really not so much for the sake of the apples—at the most I eat three apples a year, without the peel, but for the sake of my own security. In the eyes of certain parents it might look as if I cultivate apples in order to lure the children. I'm not much for running out and shouting: Get out of there, you rotten kids. I would much rather say: Just go ahead and eat. That's what apples are for. But that would be a sophisticated form of suicide.

Recently I was down at the printers with the last things for the next issue of the paper, and when I come back, the youngsters are in full swing plundering my Cox-orange tree. I act out the usual comedy, swinging my arms and acting tough, and they scatter to the four winds. Only a little girl in a light blue dress keeps standing there, Nina, the neighbor's girl, a very pretty and fairly spoiled child. I let my arms drop and said nothing. She stood staring at me with a big apple in her hand. I wondered: Should I now say: Take the apple with you and get lost—no, that wouldn't do. Drop that apple—no, I couldn't get myself to do that either. Then she solved the problem by bending forward and laying the apple in the grass. Thereupon she curtsied with both hands at the hem of her dress and said, Excuse me—and ran out of the yard.

I couldn't say anything. Should of course have shouted: Remember to keep away from now on. But that's easier when they're in a group.

But it was a very dangerous path I had taken. Suppose the girl, Nina, became suspicious that Fats Olsen wasn't as dangerous as was believed. Suppose she, the next time we met, dared to come a tiny step closer, began to talk with me, ask me about something; how long would I be able to keep her at arm's length, say that I don't have time, that she must ask her mother and father that, etc. That my anxiety was not exaggerated will be evident from the following. First it was a matter of stealing the march on her, so the next time Thorkildsen came into the shop I said: The children were in my garden again, swiping apples yesterday. And I won't have it. I'm telling you this because Nina was with them this time.

Thorkildsen had bought a pack of cheroots and was about to fish a tenspot out of his wallet, had it already half out, but stopped short, as if he regretted it. Then he cautiously pulled it all the way out and laid it slowly and carefully down on the counter.

"Was she . . ."

"Yes, but I think it's the first time, and the last, hopefully. She was the only one that apologized, by the way. I've spoken with the other parents along the way, but it doesn't help. It's damned well not so much for the sake of the apples, there are enough of them, and I hardly ever eat apples—but they are not satisfied with merely picking apples—they absolutely have to climb up in the tree and break the branches and twigs. It's a pity for the tree." A tree is also a kind of person, I was about to say.

I gave him his change for the ten. He stared at the money without touching it: "Couldn't you get a lock put on the gate?"

"Ah, what would be the use of that—the bigger boys will just hop over the fence anyway—and a lock like that is alot of bother. You don't have a lock on your gate, either, do you?"

At last he lifted his head and looked at me.

"No—why should I—I don't have any apple trees."

We stared into each other's eyes. As a sailor, I got sharp at poker, worked up a technique to keep from blinking for up to a minute. Often

39

a blink could be decisive. No, so long as we just played this game I wasn't nervous—here I knew I was superior to the other stay-at-homes, and now it even amused me to play for high stakes.

"Perhaps you would have me cut down my tree to get some peace from the youngsters?"

Thorkildsen blinked for the first time. I hadn't yet blinked, and I could easily manage at least twenty seconds more. The technique consists of the following: Just before you know it will begin, you squeeze your eyelids in tightly on the sly, while you turn your eyeballs in all directions, or you simply blink slowly a half-dozen times. With that, the eye is lubricated so it can manage a longer drying out. But now there comes a period where you, in the beginning in any case, come to blink many times quickly, each after the other, possibly because the pupils have to adjust themselves to the light after having been covered by the eyelids for several seconds. As a rule this period lasts 15-20 seconds at the start; later you can work up to, or more correctly said, down to 5-10 seconds. It is only now that you can fix your opponent's stare, so of course it depends on timing it correctly. When you begin the staring period, you pinch your eyes half together, by which the evaporation from the eye's surface is reduced and that's a great advantage, especially in intense light and tobacco smoke. If you're a beginner and are afraid of not being able to hold out long enough, there are different tricks you can use to get your opponent to blink first: it will, for example, confuse him if you don't look him directly in the eyes, but just a few millimeters to the side, or at his eyebrows, which will quickly get him to blink. Or you can let yourself squint just a little bit.

Thorkildsen blinked again and lost, this game in any case. He picked up his change and walked toward the door.

"I'll speak to Nina."

I couldn't resist following up my success and making him still more insecure.

"But don't be too harsh with her now—I just think that she is far too sweet a girl to let herself be lured into anything by the big louts."

He turned in the doorway and looked at me for a moment. It was, to put it mildly, a grudging glance, but at the same time confused. I rubbed my hands when he was gone. This was the way it should be. So long as they didn't know where I stood, I could sleep in peace. But heaven help me the day that they fancy they know it. Or if one day a crime against one of the children is really committed. Then I know well enough to whom they will first direct the attention of the police. If they even take the time to go to the police first.

One day I saw Nina walking with her grandfather along the path at the edge of the woods. They stopped now and again. When the grandfather had anything of interest to say, he bent down over her and pointed with his cane at a tree or a bird. They took each other by the hand and walked on. A little later he picked her up in his arms and gave her a kiss on the cheek and set her down again—she had already gotten big and heavy since the last time, he probably said.

You can well imagine how it would be taken if I was the one who walked hand in hand with Nina and kissed her on the cheek. Grandfather may well do it because he is normal. He has demonstrated that by, among other things, becoming a grandfather. And the funny thing is that I can really understand the parents' attitude. It's absolutely clear to me that Thorkildsen must act towards me the way he does—perhaps I would react the same way if I had children. And because it's clear to me, maybe this can be my salvation. But if I weren't accustomed to using the inside of my head more than Thorkildsen and the others usually do, if I didn't care to take the trouble to project myself into the mentality of others, if I behaved more straightforwardly and didn't take all the safety precautions that I now do, where would I be then?

If I had children. Yes, my mother—and father, if he had lived—could have been grandmother and grandfather. Perhaps great

41

grandparents. Then I'd be grandfather and could walk freely in the woods with my grandchildren by the hand. Yes, my own kid by now would have gotten somewhat bigger than Nina, nearly thirty, not easy to take up in your arms. But just about thirty years ago our daughter was cut into pieces with some kind of poultry shears or other in order to save her mother's life. Naturally the doctors meant well enough, but when they came into the waiting room and explained to me why they had carved up the child, and that they regretted that my wife had not survived the birth anyway, yes, then I was not so amenable to reason and explanations as I have later become. It was too much at once for a young fellow who had only been married eight months. It's the only time that I have struck other people, and I still regret it. It took five men to hold me. Many years later I met one of the doctors by chance, and I offered him my wholehearted apology and he took it very nicely. Moreover, he had the reputation of being a skillfull doctor.

That was why I went to sea. I had a good job in the kitchen at the Palace Hotel, but I quit. It was as if I had to get away from everything for a little while. I met other women, but it never came to anything, as a matter of fact. I was afraid of wreaking the same havoc again. I went in for poker.

When I want to find a subject for my next philosophizing corner in the paper, I usually take a walk along the path on the edge of the woods. It's good for a man of my age and weight to move his legs, and the excercise makes the blood circulate more quickly, and the brain gets an increased supply of blood, and the blood gets increased oxygen because of the more vigorous breathing. The brain becomes like a silo full of thoughts and ideas. The difficult thing is to sort out the best idea and then hold onto it, hurry back to the room and not budge until the article is finished. Saturday or Sunday afternoon I write my philosophical corner so that the printer can have it on Monday, and then I have Monday and Tuesday to finish the rest of the material, in between taking care of customers—you don't need much concentration for that kind of thing.

The path along the edge of the woods is advantageous to me in many ways. In the first place, the site. If you stand on the path with the woods on your right, you have on your left first some fields and stretches of grass with a few elder bushes and cow parsnips and behind them the outskirts of the town, suitably far enough away not to be a distraction, and the outermost houses suitably far enough so that from them an eye can be kept on whatever happens on the path if necessary. It's a great relief for me to know that they can see where I stand—purely bodily, I mean—that I'm not doing anything shady, as long as I'm walking here, anyway. For that reason I seldom go into the woods itself. It is a beautiful woods, incidentally. The terrain is very rolling and varied; dry and moist quickly alternate so that there is an exceptional mixture of all sorts of trees and kinds of birds. On weekdays the whole region is crawling with natural history classes from the whole country. But Saturday and Sunday there's no one in the woods. Ever since the democratization of the automobile, woods have again become what they were a few hundred years ago, peaceful stretches where only the hunter and the solitary wanderer roam.

Of the other advantages for me I can mention the air, which is far more pure and full of fragrance here than on the road where my house is. Even on a breezy spring day there is always an acrid smell of gasoline, burned rubber, warm asphalt, bus diesel, distant factory smoke etc., whereas the fragrance of the trees and the smell of the forest floor, and later of yarrow, burdock, and wild chervil along the path help supply to the air you breathe in those brain vitamins that make your thoughts flower. Unless you get hay fever. And then the quiet. No cars or motorbikes, just a few voices, a single courting couple, an old couple on a bench, a couple of children playing. I don't count that as noise, but as expanded silence, blossoming silence, I would surely write, if it were

43

for the dear old rag—along with the sound of birds, the hum of the trees and the flies and the dragonflies' crackling flight nearly a form of music. I must admit, however, that I am completely unmusical so maybe that's just baloney. And lastly, the very quality of the path itself. It is laid out on ancient forest floor and even though it is leveled and cleared of remains of roots you might stumble over, it has preserved its resilient quality that, sort of, lifts you farther at every step, something on which we old and weighty ones set great value. Asphalt is soft to walk on, too, but flaccid, like a worn-out spring, which gives up helping pedestrians over a certain weight class. It's something of the same thing with gravel, and flagstones act just like brakes with me—it's like being slapped underfoot with a bat at every step: back where you came from, you fat pig! I get corns and blisters and sore thighs. Flagstones are suitable only for lightfooted people and children. Dogs and sparrows, maybe.

Around four on Saturday I was finally finished with tallying the day's receipts and with the last latecomers. Some of my customers don't get out of work until one or two and take quite a while to get home so they have permission to go around to the back until about four if they have forgotten to purchase something. After that time, I've said, there was no guarantee I'd be home. I have to have a little weekend, too.

I slammed the door shut and went out to the edge of the woods. That takes twenty minutes at my tempo. But then, too, I was surrounded by colors and oxygen and birdsongs and impulses right and left. And I had the whole path to myself at that, as far as I could see.

My intention this time was to write something about apparent progress. External progress at the expense of inner. Reaction camouflaged as progress. Or: Are the Middle Ages entirely over? It should almost be a continuation of the lynching article. The difficulty lay in that there were far too many things that I wanted to include, our relationship to the developing countries, different opinions on tabus, tolerance in theory and practice, are we hopelessly provincial without even knowing it, and so forth. Maybe I would have to write a third article to get it all in, but then I'd surely have to put a more harmless article in between No. 2 and 3, or not harmless, perhaps harmful as a matter of fact, just as long as it dealt with something that I know all of us can be harmed by, e.g. oil pollution on our beaches. Then they would all come, Thorkildsen in the lead, and thank me warmly for my contribution—the right word at the right time! And satisfied each will go his way and the oil will still lay there floating along the coast. A harmful article which in its effect was completely harmless—that would have to be my next article. I would have to concentrate on this apparently harmless rigamarole for the time being.

I reached the point where the path bent and gradually disappeared into the woods. I usually turned back here so I could still be seen from the backs of the outermost houses, a few hundred meters away. I imagined that an observer sat in every house and spied on me with the aid of field glasses. That they kept in constant telephone contact with each other, relieved each other through the afternoon so that they could take turns keeping lookout and drinking coffee. Perhaps they had already appointed someone section leader—before very long they would come round to uniforms and badges, secret codes and training programs. I was just about to wave to them, but no, that would disrupt their whole tactic—they would have to call the group together hastily for consultation and then in the course of the next week they would dig observation posts out in the fields and procure field telephones so that they could keep each other oriented concerning my movements. So they would lie there then, camouflaged with grass in their hair and clover behind their ears, with their field glasses wrapped up in bindweeds and harebells. No, it got far too complicated, so I abstained from waving and began wandering back along the edge of the woods. And suddenly I got and idea about how I could sneak up on the subject. The introduction should simply be camouflaged, something like: Why don't we walk in the woods any more? Simultaneous with the increase in leisure and the improved traffic connections, the woods are depopulated—and then little by little touch upon the psychic expense of progress so that people think that they know where I stand—oh, he's a little old-fashioned and reactionary, and then put the surprising counter-maneuver in: reaction flourishes among us, the most dangerous reactionary point of view at that, those who claim to be far-sighted and tolerant, but who in reality cultivate the narrowest interests—no, that sounded a little too political—who in reality, who in their heart of hearts, yes, that was better, who in their heart of hearts would spare no pains—no that doesn't work—who in their hearts—well, the main thing was I had gotten ahold of the right angle—it was just a question of hurrying home and finding the right wording. I increased my pace and was just about to begin whistling, looking neither to one side nor the other now, but there was something or other in the woods that I must have perceived out of the corner of my eye, something bright which moved. When I looked, I saw a light blue dress, that moved among the tree trunks. Nina. I continued on but slowed down a little to consider what I should do now. Naturally I could just go on home and write my article—she would probably soon come out onto the path again. I sat down on a bench. There was no one else on the path, but I took it for granted that those over in the houses had seen both me and the girl. If I went into the woods after her, the whole alarm system would go into effect. If I called to her, she might get scared and run off in panic when she saw Fats Olsen. And yet, now, she hadn't panicked at all in the yard at home. On the other hand, there is something strange about a woods, and in any case I risked having her tell them at home that Fats Olsen had called to her. Goddammit that parents can't look after their children better. I had to hope that the people in the houses had seen Nina go into the woods and had called her parents so that one of them would soon come running. At any rate, they couldn't prohibit me from being on the path. But perhaps they'd upbraid me, then, for not having called to her and fetched her out. Better that. She was picking heather and moved gradually farther and farther away from the trunks, where there were more and more flowers. All she needed was the little red riding hood and the basket for grandmother to make the picture complete. Here sat the wolf, getting stiffer and stiffer from fright—if only the hunter would hurry up and forestall it. Eventually she disappeared from my sight. I knew that it wasn't so terribly far to the first treacherous ponds. So, they'll get me anyway, I thought, and went into the woods.

First there is a broad belt of huge aged beeches with a good distance between the trunks, luxurious space, but a few hundred meters farther in and you are in a lower growth of very mixed character, birches, small firs, larch, tiny stretches with raspberry, other tiny stretches with heather, of all things, a few blueberry or blackthorn. I thought I could remember about where the raspberries were to be found from the few walks I had dared to take in here. Perhaps Nina had happened to think of the raspberries from last summer when she had walked in here with her grandfather. And became disappointed when she discovered that it was already past raspberry season. I reached the raspberry patch and saw that she wasn't there, which made me glad in a way, since my body is unfit for forcing itself through vegetation of that thickgrowing, pricking kind. She couldn't have gone far. On the other hand, she could have gone either to the left, to the right, or straight ahead, or diagonally to the right or diagonally to the left, or she could have gone in an arc away from my path and gotten out among the beeches again. I chose to go diagonally to the right because that was the most dangerous direction—it lead to the first treacherous pool. And quite correctly. She was standing in a little glade watching a large anthill of firneedles with her back half-turned toward me.

First and foremost it was a question of her not catching sight of me too suddenly and perhaps run in panic farther in toward the dangerous area, so I hurried behind the nearest tree, a birch. Actually, it's seldom that I laugh aloud. Although I'm not devoid of a sense of humor, I'm satisfied with chuckling a little to myself whenever I read or experience something funny. But when it occurred to me that I was standing there trying to conceal my swelling body behind a delicate birch tree, which must have nearly looked like a white stripe in my clothes, then I had difficulty controlling myself. Afterwards I thought: Maybe that was the last time you had an opportunity to laugh, and you didn't even allow yourself that. Oh, well, one must be allowed a *little* self-pity in my situation, in small doses. At most, three per day. More poison and dull the organism.

I ducked into some thickets that provided pretty good cover, found a dry branch and tossed it so that it flew behind her and landed in the thicket a little to her right. Naturally it was my intent that she would be frightened and hurry off in the right direction. But when the naive girl heard the rustling sound, she started going toward the place in order to see what it was. I was just about to hit myself—I should have remembered how she reacted at the apple tree when the others bolted. I should have acquainted myself with her mode of reaction as I had done with that of her parents. Now she headed right in the direction of the pond, and I had to make an outflanking maneuver in a hurry in order to cut her off. I must have looked interesting as I rolled off with swinging arms, all the while stumbling over roots and tiny stumps, but I made it down to the pond without greater injury, halted at the very last moment with my belly half out over the water's surface—that's the insidious thing about the pond, it's hidden behind a very small border of low rushes. You don't discover it until you have one foot out over the waterlilies. I caught my breath. Yes, really, why not lean forward a little and settle down between the carp and the tench, a silent and cool

48

existence away from the hell that awaited me. My heart felt like a pent-up churchbell banging back and forth. I wheezed to recover my breath, and then the sweat began to gush down over my eyes, down behind my ears, down my thighs. But at least I got there first; I could see that the water was completely still when I dried the worst of the sweat out of my eyes. No bare spots in the duckweed. A dragonfly or a damselfly made a long detour around me. Yes, excuse me for being in the way. Now the only thing was to wait for the little girl. Just as I was going to look back there was a rustling behind me. This time I was just about to lose my balance. I got my paunch around quickly, and there she stood, with big eyes and her hand in front of her mouth.

I tried to suppress my snorting breath and look unruffled.

"So, it's you," I said. "Are you allowed to go this far into the woods?"

She quickly made a curtsy. "I can't find my way back," she said timidly. Now I could see that she had been crying. She had scraped a knee, and there was quite a considerable tear in her dress. That was all I needed.

"Did you fall?"

"Yes, I fell over a big branch that I couldn't see—and I've scratched myself on some thorns, too—look."

She showed me one of her underarms—there were three long scratches; oh yes, that was good enough, bloodshot sex criminal, who tears away at his defenseless victim.

"Listen now: you go straight ahead that way, and then you come to some birch trees. Just walk through them and then you can't miss the big trees, you know, that grow along the path. Then hurry home to your mother and get some bandaids." Her eyes began to water: "Yes, but I can't find it, and father will be so angry. . ."

"Then he should make sure to take better care of you. Well, then, I'll have to go with you and explain it. You walk ahead, I'll follow you and give directions."

She turned half-way around in the direction I pointed, put a finger in her mouth.

"Come on," I said. She misunderstood and came to me and wanted to take my hand.

"No, don't," I said and pulled my hand away. "I have a blister."

I gave her a gentle nudge in the right direction and followed a few steps behind her. I thought: well, you can start the hunt then and get it over with.

When we reached the birches she turned around once and smiled. I smiled back. I permitted myself to smile. The little spoiled kid, who for some reason or other wasn't afraid of Fats Olsen, who wanted to take him by the hand. Who smiled right at him. And got Fats Olsen to smile back. Who got Fats Olsen to feel completely outing-happy even though he knew the net was closing in on him.

"Just keep walking now," I said. "I'll be right behind you." We walked through the birch grove, came out on a little bare spot, when Nina suddenly stood still; a moment after she slowly took a few steps backward. Just then I heard right nearby a whistle and a little after a shout: "Here they are!"

Farther away other voices sounded: "Where?" "We're coming!" "Stay where you are!" "Shout again!"

Then I caught sight of the man who had called. He stood among the tree trunks just twenty meters away, stood completely stiff and stared at us. It was Christensen the house painter, also one of my customers. Nina turned and looked at me. I said: "Just stay where your are. Your father's coming soon."

Then they came from all sides, ten or twelve of them. It was Saturday afternoon, of course. The warning system must have worked perfectly—it finally proved to be justified.

One of the last to show up was Nina's father, Thorkildsen. He didn't have a big stick in his hand like many of the others. His face was completely rigid.

"Nina!" he commanded, and she walked slowly over to him.

"What's happened, what has he done?"

Nina was naturally frightened by all the sinsiter men and her stern father, so she began to cry and couldn't get a word out. Thorkildsen got down on his knees and began to examine her bruises and scratches—he didn't take any time to comfort or calm her, no, what counted most of all was to ascertain and corroborate. In a way that he obviously thought was discreet, he also took a peek under her dress. Now she was crying loudly and wanted to go home to her mother. Simultaneously the ring closed in around me. They were all fathers of families on my street, and they sent me some very lovely glances.

"He should be castrated, the pig!" hissed a voice behind me. I knew the voice—it was Madsen from the gasoline station. I couldn't help turning around and saying:

"By the way you haven't paid your bill for the last three months, Madsen. Isn't it about time? Do your customers get credit?"

Perhaps I had figured tht would take the wind out of him, but he clenched his fists, screwed up his eyes, and leaped on me. Madsen, otherwise a really nice and easy going fellow, never a bad word about anyone. He was somewhat smaller than me so all I needed to do was take a step forward and push with my belly so that he sat down and looked very surprised. It was an easy victory, but in response the others came to life. From every side they grabbed hold of my arms and tried to twist them behind my back and at the same time I was struck in the head with a branch which broke. It didn't hurt much, but I said: "Find yourself a better stick." Then I dropped to my knees and tossed the two others up over my shoulders so that they landed on top of Madsen, who was about to get up on his feet. There were still seven or eight of them on their feet, but they hesitated a little so I had time to say: "I'd prefer

51

not to hurt you."

Just then Thorkildsen arrived with a firm grip on Nina's arm. She hid her face in her other arm and sobbed loudly.

"Stop that," he shouted. "Obviously nothing really serious has happened. We got here in time. You, Pedersen, follow Nina home so the rest of us can get to the bottom of this."

When Nina had left with Pedersen, who clearly enough was not very happy about missing a little healthy lynching. Thorkildsen turned toward me and asked me with a very stiff upper lip:

"May we hear your explanation then, Olsen?"

"I will not speak under pressure. If someone is accusing me of something, let it be the business of the police to interrogate me."

Thorkildsen loosened his jaw muscles a little:

"You're not under pressure—we're asking you in a general way."

"I'm not under pressure? Then what do those sticks mean?"

"Okay," Thorkildsen said to the others "we don't need the sticks."

They threw away their sticks, that is to say, they let them drop down right at their feet.

"Good," Thorkildsen said, "so let's hear about it."

"Wonderful," I answered. "The explanation is that you gentlemen obviously are so busy washing your cars, and the gentlemen's wives are so busy blabbering on the telephone, that there obviously isn't anyone to look after your rotten kids."

One of the men bent down rapidly for his stick.

"Drop that stick!" I shouted.

He stood half bent over and looked at me doltishly.

"I said drop it!" I repeated. I could sense myself that I didn't look very nice.

The man looked at Thorkildsen. Thorkildsen said: "Drop it, now."

The man dropped it.

"What did you actually expect, anyway," I said, and I think I spoke rather loudly now. "Did you expect that I would fall down on my knees, or that I would try to take off, or that I would say: 'I'll cross out all your credit if you will let me go?' If that's what you're waiting for, then you will come to wait out your time."

Some of the men ground their teeth in anger. I heard one behind me say to his neighbor: "By God, he"ll get the starch taken out of him!"

Thorkildsen waved him off and turned to me, but he was ready to explode himself, I could see. He hissed: "Now you're going too far, Olsen. I can't vouch for what will happen if you keep on provoking us. We are, after all, eleven to one. But you get another chance—tell us what has happened with Nina."

I looked at Thorkildsen and was about to yield. I could easily understand their agitation. I could put myself in their place, but in me they just saw a perverse, unorthodox fellow. I was on the point of explaining and defending myself, but luckily I didn't lose my head. Everything that I would say would be immediately doubted or misunderstood; that I could see clearly in these faces, which to a great degree revealed their mood.

"Why don't you ask the girl," I said.

Thorkildsen clenched his teeth for a moment. Then he tried to smile. I must say that I began to gain respect for him. He was trying to be fair.

"Well, she isn't here—and she wasn't able to say a word—she was in shock. . ."

"Yes, Christ, I can well believe it!"

"Watch it now," he flared up, "What do you mean by that?"

"I simply mean that if I were a little girl, by God, I'd also go into a state of shock at seeing ten, twelve sinister men coming at me from all sides with knobby sticks."

"Careful of what you're saying!" screamed Thorkildsen. Some of the men picked up their sticks again.

"By Christ, I've been careful long enough about what I've said," I shouted. "From now on you get it full blast."

"No, don't do that! Stop. . ." Thorkildsen was red in the face from having to keep order on all sides. "Throw away those sticks I said!" He turned to me: "Well, you won't answer, then, and we have no right to force you to answer. But then you must take the consequences. You'll come with us."

"No," I answered, "or you'll have to carry me then. It suits me fine. My legs are tired from running about in the wood after Nina. Go ahead and carry me."

No one moved.

"Well," I said, "then I suggest that you gentlemen follow me home to the store. and if anyone wants to buy a beer, it will be *cash* today."

I simply began to walk, and the others rallied around me. Some of them naturally felt called upon to walk fairly close at my side, but then I accidently happened to bump into them, so they learned to keep their distance. But how would all of this have gone if I had been small and delicate and not very smart?

When we came to the first street it was completely still and deserted. Just a single frightened woman's head or two peeked from behind the curtains. When we swung around the corner to the street where the shop is, a woman came racing out of her house, grabbed her skiproping daughter by the arm, and nearly shovelled her into the entry and slammed the door.

It was not until I put the key into the shop door that it occurred to me that it was a terrible mistake I had made in inviting them home with me. But there was no way out now. I let us in. I walked behind the counter and slammed the leaf of the counter behind me. I tried to appear calm, but I was noticeably more uneasy about the situation than I was out in the woods. Since we had left the woods, no one had uttered a word.

The beer stood on shelves along one of the side walls, that is, half of the cases were behind the counter and half in front, so that people could choose their own wares. I always tried to stock beer from all the breweries in the country, both pilsner and strong beer, Albani, Fyrkat, Hobbie, Top, Silkebock, Red Erik, Havskum, etc. A lot of customers thought it looked festive to have so many different kinds of beer on the table. It could give rise to a great deal of conversation.

Madsen from the gas station was the first one to take a beer, a Buur.

"Does anyone have an opener?" he said. People began rooting around in their pockets but he continued without pausing by asking me: "Maybe you have a beer opener, Olsen?"

I took the church key out: "First the money."

It got very quiet. A few of them had moved over to the shelves with the beer but stopped now. Madsen held the bottle out with two fingers just under the cap.

"Is there so much hurry about the money—I'm really thirsty from running around in the woods."

"Two crowns and thirty, cash, please."

Madsen let go of the bottle which fell on the floor and smashed into pieces. "Oh," he said with a doltish grin and winked at the others. "It slipped. I guess I'd better take another."

He took another, an elephant beer this time, and held it up the same way between two fingers.

"How much was that you said," he asked, raising his eyebrows.

"That will be two times two crowns thirty, plus thirty ore for the bottle, which is four crowns ninety."

He dropped the bottle.

"Then it's five crowns and twenty," I said, "Cash."

The others, grinning, stepped to the side because of the glass and the splashing beer. Madsen put out his arm and ripped a row of bottles to the floor.

"Wow," he said, surprised, "how much can that be, including the bottles, too?"

I flung the opener right into his eye.

"So open the beers and drink them for Christ's sake," I shouted.

I don't remember very much of what happened next, just confusion. Some of them jumped over the counter and pitched into me, others ransacked the shelves, the bottles flew through the air, I slammed a few heads together—it sounded sickening—then I got a bottle in the head. When I came to, I was lying on the floor, coughing, and blood was running down into my throat. I opened my eyes and saw Thorkildsen bending down over me. He had something in his hand, the upper half of a bottle he had broken on the counter. He waved the stump of the bottle right above my head.

"Out with it," he shouted.

A few of the others tried to calm him down.

I sat up. A few helpful gentlemen helped me all the way to my feet.

The shop was simply smashed to pieces. The counter was overturned. Cigarettes, pieces of glass, Donald Duck comics, razorblades everywhere. The floor swam in sherry, beer, and port. My back was soaking wet. They had also taken loving care with my back room—my papers lay scattered all about in the mess. The gentlemen stood around me with their hands at their sides—only a few of them sat on the overturned counter and drank schnapps out of a bottle, Brondum.

Blood ran out of my hair and over my forehead and tickled my eyes.

"Ask your daughter," I said.

"Come on, or I'll . . ." he fenced with the bottle stump. "She won't say anything."

I wiped the blood from my face and said: "If you used these methods on her, she'd tell you anything."

Then two things happened at once. Thorkildsen, who was still being held tightly by his previously so willing henchmen, managed to hurl the bottle at me anyway. It whistled right pass my ear and smashed right next to the door, and at the same time the two belltones rang that signify the shop door is opening. It was Mrs. Thorkildsen who came in. She stopped in the doorway and stared at us, at the whole mess. A few centimeters to the left and the bottle would have struck her.

"What on earth is going on here?" she asked.

She looked up and down the line but clearly had a hard time catching anyone's eye so she turned to me:

"I just want to say thank you for helping Nina find her way. She says that she met you all the way down by Black Pond."

I nodded politely and answered: "Yes, that's right. But try to watch her a little better in the future."

She stared at me, at the others, at her husband, at the floor, at the entire havoc.

"I'll certainly do that," she said, and left. Kling-klong the doorbell said again.

It got very quiet after she left. Little by little the others trickled out the door. I didn't try to detain them.

I stayed indoors all day Sunday. Cleaned up the store.

On Monday there was still a great deal to clean up, and I had to lie down every once in a while because of the pain, so I put a nice sign on the door: Closed for clean-up. I called the printer's to say that I couldn't come with the material before Wednesday at the earliest. He would have to postpone the paper for a few days. He was usually a rather irascible man but he took it remarkably well.

Tuesday I took the sign down. Sat most of the day in back and worked on the material for the paper. There were no customers.

It wasn't until half past four that the bell over the door rang. It was Thorkildsen, Madsen and two others who came in.

"What would you like, gentlemen," I asked politely.

Thorkildsen stepped up to the counter.

"We'd like to apologize for Saturday."

"Thank you," I said politely.

Thorkildsen looked a little weak-kneed. Still, he was the one who took it upon himself to speak for the other gutless wonders. I respect something like that. Perhaps he wasn't the worst father Nina could have after all. To say nothing of the mother.

"We know very well you could make a terrible mess for us—with the police and all that."

I answered: "I don't think there's anything to bother the police with now."

The gentlemen looked relieved and shifted their weight from one foot to the other.

Thorkildsen cleared his throat: "I'm also thinking more about—the havoc we created Saturday—that is the expense I mean."

"It will be on your bill," I said. "I'll try to divide it fairly."

Thorkildsen smiled and stretched out his hand: "Let's let everything be as it was then, shall we?"

I could well understand his smile, but I didn't like it. I pretended not to see his hand, began to straighten up the few bottles that were left, my back half-turned to him.

"Yes," I said, "everything is as it was."

The doorbell rang—they were on their way out. I turned around and said to Thorkildsen:

"Say hello to Nina for me. And especially to your wife."

Thorkildsen turned in the doorway and fired a look that I haven't yet been able to find words for. But in any case it wasn't friendly. He banged the door shut.

So everything is as it was. So long as they don't know where I stand, I'll make do during my time here.

I've also thought about picking the apples from the tree and putting them in a case in front of the store with a sign: 'Delicious, gratis apples for free use'. But that would be misunderstood, too. As a somewhat sophisticated allurement. No, I'll probably have to cut down the apple tree. For the time being.

The Speaking Strike

It must be hard to be born mute, to be cut off from the use of speech by a whim of nature, to use the euphemism.

Whether it is more trying, just as trying, or less trying to be forced into silence by external circumstances, political conditions, for example, is something I don't want to speculate about—I am not going to compare miseries.

But I can say that a silence neither assumed voluntarily nor borne involuntarily, a silence which is meaningless because it is justified by a meaningless idea, is a great burden for a boy with normal powers of speech and a strong desire to use them.

1

One Saturday afternoon I bicycled over to Allan's place.

I always rang the doorbell first even though I knew the bell didn't work. But every time I figured it might have been fixed since the last time.

Then I knocked. The round shape of Allan's mother filled the space occupied by the door, but for once she didn't step back to let me come in.

"If it's Allan you want, he's not at home," she said and stood in the doorway. Her small eyes were larger than usual. I could see that she had been crying.

"I just wanted to lend him this," I said and handed her a cowboy pulp magazine, *The Black Mask of the Prairie.*

She looked at the magazine without opening it, and then the tears began to roll down over her round cheeks.

This was the first time I had seen someone break into tears over a cowboy magazine. She handed it back to me and I was just about to take it when she suddenly grabbed it and pressed it to her huge bosom.

"I hope you have never hit your mother in the head with a magazine or anything else, because I don't want to think such a thing of you!"

I hadn't expected this reaction at all and didn't know what I should say, and I didn't get anything said before she went on:

"I simply asked him to wash up. I wait on him hand and foot, and what do I get for it?"

The magazine whizzed right past my ear when she flung it down the stairs.

I took a firm hold on the guardrail.

"Now it's up to his father, and you can give him that message! He's probably down in the woodshed."

Even if I had had the chance I wouldn't have had the courage to ask whether it was Allan or his father who was down in the woodshed.

She slammed the door with such a bang that the guardrail vibrated in my hand and the neighbor's terrier began to bark behind the opposite door.

I snuck down the stairs, picked up the magazine from the next to the last step and walked around behind the house, across a small yard, where laundry hung waving, and over to the woodshed.

Allan stood patching a leak in a bicycle tire. The bike stood with its wheels in the air, the inner tube on the rear wheel was yanked out like the intestines of a slaughtered animal; it was covered with countless patches, round, oval, rectangular, large and small, red and black, the lowest part of the gut lay soaking in an old water basin.

I didn't quite know how to start in on what I had just experienced. Or whether I should.

But he looked up from the water basin, pulled his upper lip back from his teeth like an aggressive chimpanzee and hissed:

"Are they green?"

I didn't understand what he meant. I glanced around. When people talked about "the green ones" it was usually the Germans they had in mind.[1] But we very rarely saw the green uniforms in Soborg,[2] and in any case there were none right there.

Allan pointed, with his front teeth still bared, at the elder trees behind the clothes line and hissed:

"THAT is green!"

He threw out his other arm and pounded his clenched fist on the open door of the woodshed:

"THAT is green!"

The green paint on the door had flaked off in several layers and you could see that it had been brown before and white before then. Still I could go along with the idea that at the moment it was green, generally speaking. But I didn't say anything, because as he stood there with bared teeth, arms jutting out at his sides, and bloodshot, vengeful eyes, I expected to see foam pour out from between his teeth at any second—I had read about rabies.

Allan lowered his arms and now pointed with both index fingers at his bare teeth:

"Are THEY green?"

I stared at his teeth, his front teeth, which were amazingly large when seen in their entirety, stark naked. They weren't pearly white,

---

[1] Denmark was occupied by German military forces from April 9, 1940 until May 5, 1945.

[2] Soborg is one of Copenhagen's northwestern suburbs.

more like yellowish. Not dull and dark yellow as with people who smoke a lot. I would call them whitish yellow, or maybe yellowish white, medium whitish yellow, with some greyish white bits of food between the very front teeth. But green? No. Still I didn't dare deny it because I knew he would become even more hysterical if I didn't agree with him if he now, damn it, had gotten it into his head that his teeth were green!

He dropped his arms. Let his upper lip fall into place. With some difficulty, because teeth get dry and rough from being in the open air too long. Now he resembled himself again, and there wasn't any foam in the corners of his mouth.

I pulled out the magazine.

The Black Mask of the Prairie and the Phantom-Stagecoach.

He looked at it wearily and said with his normal voice:

"If it had been a plate. Or the coffee pot. Or the stove!"

I didn't let on that I was understanding less and less but just asked: "What really happened?"

"She said I should brush my teeth. In a little bit, I said. I was sitting reading a magazine. She just kept at me. Finally she said my teeth were green. From mold. Then she caught the magazine in the head. A thin little magazine. If it had been a cup or plate."

She was real mad anyhow," I said, "she threatened to tell your father."

"Women are cowards," he said. "There's a real good chance she'll talk him into giving me a licking when he gets here, but that doesn't matter, he never hits hard. He *could*, but he doesn't like to. Naw, that's not what . . ."

He didn't say anything else. "That's not what." You could keep on wondering what "what" might be. That's the way he was. He left a sentence like that hanging in mid-air until someone rose to the bait. Apparently not caring *whether* anyone was crazy enough to rise to the

64

bait. Because when you knew Allan you knew how dangerous it was. And that this was the last chance to back off real quietly with the excuse that you had promised your mother to mind the shop. But for the very reason that you knew how dangerous it was and that you would probably get involved in something difficult and terrifying, something you would regret long afterwards, that was exactly what made you stay put. Because it's one thing to get caught up in something you don't want to do. But it's completely unbearable to run from something you know very well you don't want to do without yet knowing what it is.

So while Allan bent over the inner tube again, clamped his hands around it and listened to the bulge he made, I took my time. Even though I almost knew what would happen I didn't intend to give in so easily. If he wanted me in on something he would have to open his mouth himself.

I thought of the father I didn't have. I wondered if he would have given me a licking if he were alive. I tried to imagine a situation. My temporarily resurrected father comes home after a rather long voyage at sea. Mother throws herself into his arms and says: "Erling has been very bad and disobedient while you were gone—now you've got to lay down the law!"

My father looks at me. His face is just a pale oval with a friendly glow, I really don't know what he looks like. And from the nice oval come the words: "Today we're going to celebrate, not thrash—come here, my boy!" And he opens his arms.

I couldn't imagine anything else.

2

Allan let half the air out of the inner tube and let the bald tire eat it up a little bit at a time. He worked with experienced movements, patching bicycle tires was a daily task in those days. At intervals he gradually pumped the tube up and pounded out the tire with the shaft of a screwdriver. When he was all finished he gave the wheel a gentle slap to make it whirl around.

"What time is it now?" he asked. Neither of us had a watch on.

"It's probably two-thirty," I said, "maybe a quarter of."

"Good," he said, "in a bit, from three o'clock on we're going on a speaking strike, twenty-four hours to start with."

"What do you mean?" I asked in surprise.

"We won't say a word to anybody from now until three o'clock tomorrow afternoon. Not a word. No matter what they say or do to us. Then they can try and see what that tells them."

"What do you mean *we*?"

"Just you and me. At first I thought about having Ove in on this. But he's too soft, he can't keep his trap shut for two minutes."

I did feel a little proud to be counted one of the tough, silent elite, but I was actually more confused.

"Okay, but why me, your mother didn't do anything to me, I didn't do anything to her, and my mother doesn't have anything at all to . . ."

"It isn't just that," he broke in. He pressed the patched tire and slapped it for a couple more whirring twirls.

"That's part of it, of course, but not just that," he continued. "But who is it who decides everything? Is it us? Who decides that you should mind the kiosk—is it you yourself?"

I had never viewed my afternoon hours in the shop that way. I thought it was exciting to browse around among the magazines and newspapers, to talk with people and take money. I was almost honored that Mother allowed me to do it. It made me feel grownup. But then I remembered last Thursday, when it was very warm and I would rather have gone swimming. It was exactly that day that it was especially important that I mind the shop because Mother was going to the hairdresser. I was real mad so now I understood quite well what Allan meant. But still . . .

"They have the say in everything, they decide everything we have to say, thanks for the meal, and yes, I'll take the garbage out, mother dear, and brush my moldy teeth, and I will do my homework right away. And at school—damn, it's Sunday tomorrow—can't you just see us in a speaking strike during class!"

I could see it very clearly, I was relieved that tomorrow was Sunday, the whole thing was unpredictable enough as it was.

"If we manage twenty-four hours we can add an extra day," he said thoughtfully.

"One day is enough!" I hurried to say, more than enough, in fact.

"But there's one thing they can't decide!" He tried to ring the bicycle bell. It made a couple of choked clicks, the lid was jammed down from the bike having been stood upside down. "They can't decide when we will open our mouths or not. They can't force us to speak. Can they force you?"

"No, no!" I said spontaneously and added "but it'll be a little hard to explain to Mother . . ."

"Damn it, you're not going to explain anything! *That's* what I'm talking about!"

Okay. So that's what it was about.

"We don't need to excuse ourselves for not saying a peep for a day. It's not against the law. Is it written somewhere that you absolutely *have to* keep your jaw moving for twelve hours? We just studied the Constitution. There's something there about freedom of speech and freedom of expression. If the idea had been that nobody was allowed to keep their mouth shut, then there would be something about *required* speech and *required* expression."

In all the time I had known Allan I had never heard him use so many words in connected speech. It was as if the very thought of silence gave him diarrhea of the mouth.

"That's exactly what I'd like to explain to Mother," I said, "then she would be better able to understand . . ."

"Afterwards!" he shouted, "afterwards you can explain the whole thing, she can certainly wait that long, can't she stand suspense?"

"I have a better idea," I said. "It's all right for you to go on a speaking strike because you feel you're being treated unfairly. But you yourself know very well that you go for several hours without saying boo, people are used to that. Your own father calls you 'the silent Dane.' Not a soul will notice that you're on strike. What I mean is that it won't cost you anything! Not so with me. Mother says I chatter like a monkey. If I'm quiet she would just say: 'Well, now a body has a chance to hear one's own thoughts!' "

Allan squinted his eyes and let go with that contemptuous snort I normally did everything to avoid. But this time I stood fast because I was certain he couldn't shoot holes in these arguments.

"I thought you said you had a *better* idea," he sneered. And I thought: In a minute he's going to spit on the ground, but I'll stand pat!

His way of talking reminded me of the scene where the Black Mask of the Prairie is facing Billy Scarface, one of the worst desperados in the West, and Scarface says contemptuously to the crowd in the saloon:

"I thought I heard someone here in the saloon mumble something about me having to be out of town before midnight if I valued my life— did I hear that right?"

So I answered Allan just as Black Mask answered Scarface:

"You heard dead right!"

"And what is that 'idea' all about?" As he said it he worked his mouth from side to side so as to collect a real repulsive wad of spit.

"The idea is that *you* will go on strike and *I* will go around and tell everybody why you won't say anything!"

He stopped moving his mouth and stared at me stonily. I continued.

"And I'll also explain to them that if they don't treat you better you are prepared to continue your speaking strike for a week. A month even, if it has to be!"

The incredible thing happened that Allan for the first time opened his eyes wide. In any case I had never seen his eyes so large that you could see the whites all the way around the blue. He made a sound so I believed for a moment he had swallowed the spit and was about to choke on it. But that lasted for only a second, then his eyes became small and hard again. He turned toward the green, peeling door. A big blowfly sat there rubbing its hands together. Allan was undefeated in the long-distance spit so I wasn't a bit surprised when an instant later the fly slid backward down the door, enveloped in the biggest glob of spit seen in Frederiksborg County to date. And even though I stood across from the fly I knew for certain that I had missed a similar fate by only the skin of my teeth.

Allan turned toward me. He had apparently shaken off what had been bothering him. Suddenly looked completely friendly. Came over and placed a hand on my shoulder. Was on the verge of saying something but then glanced up at the windows to see if anyone was listening. Drew me into the farthest corner of the yard where no one could hear us. Spoke in a very low voice without moving his lips, with a catlike purr in his throat, which he did when he spoke of extremely secret things:

"I'm not saying that your idea isn't good. I understand completely what you have in mind with it. But it just can't be used here, you see. Because. First and foremost it's a matter of driving them crazy with curiosity so they'll do anything to learn what's going on. But they'll learn that only afterward, when they've given in—do you follow me?"

I nodded and suppressed a yawn. Every time he talked in that purring way I felt like under hypnosis. I felt a great need to yawn and lie down in a corner and fall asleep on the spot. But I knew he would be hurt if I yawned now. So I pressed my lips together and yawned *inwardly*, so to speak. I felt my neck become twice as thick, and I'm certain my ears stuck out from my head at ninety-degree angles. That's why I could only answer with a 'huung' through my nose.

He gave me a quick look, and I forced myself to smile in agreement.

"Good," he purred, "and secondly, it will be a test for us, too."

My ears were pounding. I was certain that the high inner pressure would in a moment either burst my eardrums or stretch them out like balloons, so I decided to let a little of it out through the corner of my mouth. It sounded about like someone stepping on a half-empty bagpipe.

Allan looked at me suspiciously.

"What's the matter?"

"Nothing, just a belch, what do you mean, test?" I hurried to take a couple of breaths so I got rid of the old air because I still needed to yawn.

Allan continued in his low hum:

"Some say the war will soon be over. Others say it'll last for another three or four years yet. Do you realize what that means?"

Even though I didn't understand completely I nodded with tight lips and protruding ears.

"By that time we'll be seventeen or eighteen. Sooner or later we won't be able to avoid getting into something. People like you and me. And what'll happen if we get picked up?"[1]

This time I slowly shook my ears from side to side with a thoughtful expression. I was actually thinking mostly about whether I could somehow just direct the pressure downward so it could come out

[1] Anticipating the risk of being picked up by the Nazis for participation in the resistance.

in the form of a gigantic fart, or, as Allan's father said: a colossal ass tornado. That was a sport Allan himself was a master at, and he respected it, so it wouldn't even need to be explained.

"The best thing that could happen would be to be gunned down on the spot. Because if they get you under interrogation. And you're supposed to give names. They'll want me to give your name. And you to give mine. Or your mother's. Maybe your mother will be hiding parachutists at that time. And they force redhot needles under your nails. To start with. If that doesn't do it they'll take pliers and tear the nails out. They'll start with the left little finger. Repeat the questions. If you don't answer they'll take the next nail. And so on. Could you keep quiet about your mother when they reached the nail of your right thumb?"

I couldn't answer the question. At the same time I noticed that the air was seeping out of me. Not out of my nose or ears or butt, just out of my pores or however it came out. I felt very limp and didn't have the need to yawn anymore.

"And of course the finger nails aren't the end of it. You've also got toenails. And you've got teeth. And eyes. And balls."

"I've got to go home now," I said. "I should already be home."

"How could you stand it if you can't keep your mouth shut for just twenty-four hours, under normal conditions, when you've got your nails all for yourself and just need to clip them whenever you yourself want to?"

"Could you?" I asked weakly.

"That's exactly what we're going to try!" he said. "If we stick together!"

"Let's do it then," I said and tottered back to my bicycle. I would go along with everything just so I could escape now.

"We'll meet here tomorrow at three o'clock!" he called after me.

He sounded perfectly happy.

3

I raced up Dyssegaard Road, just wanted to get home quickly. But after I had turned the corner at Vangede Street, I slowed down. What would I say to Mother when I got home? Or, rather, how would I manage to not say anything. It wouldn't surprise me either if she would want me to mind the shop for an hour. Just how would I manage to explain to her that I wouldn't be able to mind the shop without opening my mouth, without saying so much as: one crown, please.

But now Ove came walking on the other side of the street. He came straight across the street waving his arms:

"It's good I ran into you—I've got something to tell you!"

I stepped hard on the pedals, looked straight ahead, and shot past him, but I heard his voice at my back:

"Hey, what's the matter? What did I do?"

I rode very fast. I was boiling inside but the sweat that ran into my eyes felt ice-cold and burned like acid.

"That's not the way to treat a friend," I mumbled to myself, and I kept on repeating it, rhythmically, like a refrain:

"That's not the way to treat a friend!"

I now realized that the task was even more difficult than I had imagined. I turned down Fraende Road, partly in order not to meet anyone I knew, partly in order to gain time before I stood in front of Mother. The refrain was changed to "that's not the way to treat your mother!" and at the same time I made a detour so as to get home later. But that wasn't enough.

I pulled up at a corner and thought about letting the air out of the front tire: "The bike had a flat tire, I had to push it all the way home . . ."

But how to explain it without words?

I tried to perfect a whistling puncture sound, so convincing that words were superfluous:

"PZZFIIUUUUOOOH!"

The first time it sounded a little tame. The second time I stretched my lips more so they were forced apart from inside by the initial PZT, but the following release of air still sounded too flabby because the lips were apart now. That's why on the third time I clamped my front teeth down onto my lower lip fast as lightning right after PZT so that the following sound was really forced out through a very small, unwilling slit:

"PZT-FF-zzzziiieeehh . . ."

or something like that.

The last part of the sound had hardly thinned out into a spitty hiss when a hand was placed on my shoulder. I leapt up, turned around and fell over my bike all at the same time.

It was a man in a gray jacket, white mason's pants, and rubber shoes. He smiled apologetically and picked up the bicycle when I had untangled myself from it.

"I wasn't trying to scare you! Were you calling your dog?"

I shook my head.

"A cat, maybe?"

I shook my head again. He looked at me for a moment.

"Well, what I really wanted to ask, I don't know this neighborhood very well, but I'll bet you do."

I had to nod yes to that. I foresaw new difficulties.

"You see, I can't find Minde Way . . ."

He stopped and began to laugh, loudly and boisterously, almost like Allan's father.

"Could you hear that?" he shouted.

I wasn't really sure what he had heard so I just looked at him. He grasped me lightly by the arm:

"I can't find Minde Way . . . no, just a second."

Suddenly he became serious, dropped my arm, and peered for a

73

moment into a hedge. Then he turned around and looked happy again:

"Now I've got it: "I can't *find my way* to *Minde Way*—what do you say?"

I smiled and nodded at him. I felt calmer now since he apparently was one of the talking sort who will take a nod or a shake of the head as an answer. But I had miscalculated, because now he said:

"Well, here I'm standing talking. Is it far from here?"

At any other moment it would have been as easy as pie for me to say:

"First straight down this street, through the first three or four intersections. Then you'll come to a little larger street, Dyssegaard Road. Right across, then the next street is Minde Way."

But just try to explain that with gestures.

First I pointed down Amindingen Road, and he nodded in the same direction. Then I began to count on my fingers for him.

He stared at me with a strangely troubled look, so I took the bike and went ahead of him down toward Minde Way. He walked a couple of steps behind me, at first without saying anything. Only after we had passed Frue Street and Hjemme Street did he say from behind:

"I've got a nephew with the same problem. Not really nephew— he's my wife's little brother, but I call him nephew. I can't bring myself to call an eleven-year-old kid 'brother-in-law'."

I sped up, I really didn't have any time for all this. On the one hand it was definitely a legal delay that you were giving someone directions. On the other hand how do you explain it to Mother with gestures?

Now he raised his voice behind me, he was almost shouting: "Can you hear what I'm saying now?"

I stiffened up from fright, but not so stiff that I couldn't speed up. What was he up to?

Nobody else was to be seen on the street. Was anyone at home in the houses? If I now were to drop the bicycle, race over and knock on a door, and if no one were at home and he followed me . . . he didn't look like that, didn't sound like that either, but isn't that exactly what's treacherous about them?

I heard him mumble: "That's just what I thought."

Suddenly he was in front of me and placed his hand on the handle bar. I stood stock-still and stared at his face.

He still looked friendly. Didn't at all look like someone who would harm anyone. Had happy blue eyes with little furrows when he smiled and didn't have a trace of a beard. Just kick them in the crotch, Allan said once. But it would be impossible for me to kick such a nice face in the crotch. If he only looked more disgusting. I searched for something really unpleasant in his face. It was hopeless, but then he helped me out. He began to contort his mouth into exaggerated, huge grimaces. He let go of the handle bar and pointed at his mouth with two straight fingers and shouted:

"He, my nephew, I mean, he goes to the Institute for the Deaf, Kapel Street or Kastel Street, do you follow me?"

Now I realized that the man probably wasn't a sex criminal but simply loony. But that just calmed me down a little bit. I kept on trying to find something repulsive about him, and now I caught sight of two long black hairs which protruded from his one nostril and moved when he talked. They reminded me of the huge spider in the woodshed at Allan's place, when it stuck its long, furry, front legs out through the opening in the corner web.

He kept on pointing at his mouth, which was changing shape all the time. First it was round, then triangular, the tongue struggled and squirmed around as if what it most wanted was to get far away immediately, just like me. He spoke so overclearly that in a way it became unclear.

"Are you fa-mil-i-ar with lip-read-ing?"

75

I shook my head.

"What a-bout sign lang-u-age?"

Allan and I often used sign language in class when we wanted to communicate something to each other which the teacher or the others shouldn't hear. Probably the most frequent sign was to place a finger on the temple and to slowly make a circle when something seemed totally idiotic to us. So I nodded yes.

Now he began to open and close his hands, to knead and massage the air, to point to the right and to the left and to thump himself on the forehead and the chest. In order to gain time I nodded yes, and at the same time got onto my bike, as if for no reason.

He stood and looked at me uncomprehendingly for a bit and thought the situation over. Then he began again to poke around in the air with his fingers and to thump his forehead.

I held up four fingers. That was supposed to mean the four streets he still had to cross. Then I pointed down the street again. He stared in that direction for a moment, and I used that time to take off as fast as I could.

I didn't look back.

He didn't call after me.

4

"Where have you been all this time?" Mother asked before the shop door had closed behind me. At first I didn't need to wrack my brain as to how I would answer because she immediately continued:

"And here I was supposed to be at the cemetery an hour ago. Now it's getting too late, it'll soon be time to fix something to eat, and meals don't make themselves. Tomorrow is Sunday and there'll be a lot of people at the cemetery."

She paused and looked at me.

"You didn't answer me. Where have you been?" I just stared at her.

"Say, can't you even answer when someone talks to you?"

I remembered my "conversation" with the man and slowly shook my head. Mother frowned.

"What's that supposed to mean? Have you lost your tongue?"

This time I nodded. So far things had gone more easily than I had expected. But Mother became nervous.

"What's wrong, son, is there something wrong with your throat, try to whisper to me at least . . ."

The silence agreement did not include whispering, not expressly, but I had the distinct feeling that it would be cheating. But clearing your throat, as if you were trying to whisper something, had to be permitted, even if just barely, so I began to clear my throat in order to gain time.

But the strenuous silence of the last hour had caused something or other to collect in my throat. I wasn't even able to clear my throat, I felt I was choking and began to cough, backwards I almost said, because it seemed the cough couldn't get out through the mouth but traveled downward and tried to punch its way out through my ribs. A big, stiff plug of phlegm blocked the way, I could neither cough it up nor swallow it, and now I couldn't breathe either. My eyes pulled down the blackout curtains in broad daylight, I sank to my knees and leaned my forehead against the back of the cash register.

Mother slapped open the flap in the counter with a bang and was at my side. She pounded on my back and held my forehead with the other hand.

"Spit it out!" she shouted, "just spit it out, I'll clean up afterwards. I don't think you've got a temperature . . ."

Her energetic pounding managed to loosen the plug. It's true it didn't come up, I got rid of it by swallowing. Finally there was a hole through it. I gasped for air, howling like a snowstorm. The gusts of air leaving and entering had a hard time passing each other in the narrow pipe, and my forehead was dripping wet under her cool hand.

"Or maybe you do have a little temperature," Mother said.

She lifted me up and supported me all the way up the stairs. In a flash she pulled off my pants and had me wrapped up in bed. I don't know how she managed to get the kettle on at the same time, but it seemed that it was whistling before my head touched the pillow, and a second later the aroma of camomile tea was there.

Camomile tea was hardly my favorite drink, but at that instant my insides felt like packed felt or ragged wool which might be soaked and softened by camomile tea. Mother supported my head while I sucked the scalding liquid in long slurps, even though I clearly heard how it grated the dried-up mucous membrane as it went all the way down. It sounded—and felt—like yanking a bandage off a wound. Or ripping skin off a flounder.

Groaning, I sank back onto the pillow. Steam hung in front of my mouth like on a clear, frosty day, and it was a while before Mother's face appeared through the fog.

I was in such sorry shape that for a moment I had forgotten the oath of silence and wanted to say something, maybe thanks. But when the boiled remains of my tongue touched the corrugated washboard of my palate, no more than a brief fizz came out, and Mother said:

"No, don't say anything now! Rest for an hour, then I'll bring some camomile tea and see how you are. Or how about a rum toddy? I've been saving a pint of Jamaica rum for several years. Actually it was meant for old Sorensen for Christmas—he's the nicest, most considerate of our customers—the others will have to settle for cheap Danish fruit wine. But we could open it and explain to him why a little had been taken, we could also invite him to dinner on Christmas Day, he doesn't have anyone. No, you mustn't say anything now, and if you don't feel better in the course of the night I'll call Dr. Christensen

78

tomorrow morning. I know it's Sunday and he'll be upset if I call him at home. But I do that so rarely. I've got a couple of real cigars—for emergency situations[1]—I put a couple potato halves in the box so they wouldn't get too dry—oh, dear, I'd better change them."

She kept on talking to me, and her eyes were covered by a glassy membrane which was both clear and murky and made me unable to look at her eyes without myself crying. So instead I looked at her hair and thought what I would say if I could have spoken, I forced myself to look at her hair and away from her eyes.

I would say "your hair is pretty, very pretty. You don't need to go to the hairdresser, it's so brown and thick and smooth and wavy and friendly. Don't get a permanent, leave it the way it is. It sure is nice that ladies don't get bald. I wish your hair will always stay as it is, always, promise me that . . ."

Mother stood up and went over to the window. She blew her nose in her careful, jerky way as if she wanted to be sure it all came out while also keeping important organs in. When she turned around, her eyes were as clear as usual.

"I can see what you're thinking. So you don't need to say anything. Just rest. And don't stick your feet out from under the comforter. I hear customers."

She left with the empty cup.

I wanted to shout: "Mother, come back, it's just a game Allan and I are playing, don't worry . . ."

Instead I stuck my head under the comforter and said, very softly but clearly, with stress on each syllable:

"Ca-mo-mile-tea."

What a relief it is to hear your own, familiar voice again!

---

[1] During the occupation, rare consumer goods could be used as barter for services and necessities.

What an experience to be allowed to say that one word!

I wrapped my arms around me, lifted my knees up to my chest, chuckled with suppressed laughter and rolled from side to side in the darkness of the comforter.

I had never known or noticed how tasty and juicy it is to pronounce the word camomile tea—in the future I would say it several times a day!

I had to find a word with different letters and experience how it felt.

"Po-lyps, po-lyps," I chanted.

That felt better yet, especially with the syllable "lyp". It had both a high and a deep sound, which caused some small vaults in my skull to echo, but at the same time it contained a special punch because of the p. I repeated it:

"Lyp-lyp-lyp!"

It reminded me of the nightingale's triadic refrain to it's more complexly ornamented melodies and trills: dyup-dyup-dyup!

I tried out several more words. Words without any noticeable connection to each other, and each one of them without a connection to the situation. I simply enjoyed them, like real chocolate and genuine chocolate covered cherries.

The previous Christmas Mother and I had shared the last real Christmas sweets she had saved up from the old days. The marzipan was dry and cracked after several years' sojourn in a cake box, and the original fluid content of the chocolate covered cherries had hardened long ago, but still how fine they tasted when dissolved in the ample and receptive water of my mouth!

I gorged myself on words like:
            chocolate covered cherries
            pickled pig's feet
            cowcatcher

green grocer
I had an orgy with words like:
water wheel
sabotage
rutabaga ragout

But my desire for pleasure wasn't satisfied, it was just strengthened. Each voluptuous utterance simply aroused my desire for even more sumptuous, more exotic dissipation. I wallowed in exquisite and fabulous word combinations:

watergreencatcher
cowpicklepie
rutabagababybuggy

Eventually it got too stuffy to breathe under the comforter, and Mother might also come up and look in on me between a couple of customers. So I sat up in bed again, and with my eyes on the door I continued for a time with words like:

soapysudssabotage
sunnysidesanddollars
flowingfountainpenfluid

I must have looked happy when Mother returned a bit later with the sweet-smelling rum toddy because she herself brightened up:

"I can see that you already feel much better! Drink this and see if you can't sleep a little. Then you'll soon be your old rambunctious self again. I put a big piece of rock candy in it, the last one I had and probably the last we'll see for a long time."

She placed the toddy on the little stool by the bed. She had poured it into a glass which she put inside a tin mug with a handle so I could drink without burning anything but my tongue, palate and insides.

This time I sipped more cautiously, but it tasted wonderful. The warmth spread from inside at the bottom of my stomach out to my skin and down to my toes. My ears began to hum, as if my brain on its own remembered an old melody. Mother's smile came closer and grew fuzzy:

"I have to go down again, but I don't think we need to call Dr. Christensen . . ."

I wanted to both laugh and cry. I was filled with glowing well-being while at the same time I tried to hold on to a feeling of remorse, like a drunken man hanging onto a lightpole.

"Still it's a pity you tricked Mother into opening the bottle of rum that was meant for old Sorensen . . ."

I didn't get all the toddy drunk before I fell asleep.

5

I sat, or lay, on a city square, or a market square. A square without houses around it but not out in the open either.

A number of people stood and looked down at me.

I could hear some ticking or clicking sounds which I could not locate, but they came from some place nearby.

I tried to get up, because I had to give a speech. But my limbs were very heavy, and when I realized I didn't have any pants on I remained lying a little while longer.

I looked up at the standing people. Couldn't really see their faces from where I was, only their green teeth and nostrils, which were big and black. Long spider legs stuck out of them. That really didn't scare me, I was more nervous about the ticking or clicking sound, which came and went.

All of them were men and they had stuck their hands into the pockets of their wrinkled, white, mason's pants. Mother was nearby, I knew, but I couldn't see her, she had to be somewhere behind the towering men.

I began my important speech, my lips moved but not a sound came out. The men bent closer over me, as if to listen, so now I could see their eyes better. But they didn't look me in the eye, they looked down on my body, at my hands and feet, maybe at my dick, so I pulled my legs up, wrapped my arms around my knees and kept on talking, but not a word was heard. What I had to say was of the greatest importance for the whole world, and I felt how I shaped my mouth into large ovals and triangles in order to pronounce clearly words I myself couldn't comprehend, except for the words "extremely important" and "camomile tea." At the same time the clicking sound became louder, and it came from their pockets. I realized that they were standing there with pliers in their pockets, and that was the reason why they were so interested in my nails and sexual organs. At the same time I heard Mother's voice, strangely tortured and unclear, as if she had a gag over her mouth: "Don't say anything now!" The clicking sounds stopped abruptly, the men raised up straight and went over to the corner where Mother's voice came from. With all my might I tried to get up, but my back and hands were greased with brown soap or some other smeary stuff, so I kept falling on my back, on one side and then the other. I wanted to scream but now my mouth was full of greasy, smeary rags which forced my tongue against my uvula. I heard Mother's voice again: "Not the nails! My hair instead!" That caused me to fix my nails in the floor like claws in order to get a firm grip. The floor or square was as soft as a mattress, but I kept my grip and was finally able to sit up.

It was half dark in the room, the drapes were drawn. But it was possible to see, it was still light outside. The wallclock was ticking. From the middle of the round face with its many number-eyes two black legs pointed sharply downward toward either side. It was five thirty-five.

I could smell dried cod from below.

I couldn't stand dried cod, but at that moment I could eat all the dried cod in the whole world and then ask for more just in order to show my gratitude that we were alive, that we were here.

I felt a hot, burning pressure behind my eyes, but I didn't cry. It was as if my tears had been transformed into words which poured from my mouth as a quiet chant or hum. The words came spontaneously, my lips moved on their own.

"Thank you, dear God, and Mother, thank you, everybody, even if you can't hear me, and Allan, too, and listen to what I have to say: a person must not be forced to be silent when he wants to talk. A person must not be forced to talk when he wants to be silent. A person should not be forced in any way, because it is bad, even if harm isn't intended. There is a time to talk and a time to be silent. That's the way it is, that's the way a person is, and each person must figure out on his own when it is time to speak and to be silent. People should not tamper with this, because it is bad, even if the intention is good. Remember this, all of you, and Allan, too. I hereby break the oath of silence I was forced to take, which I was threatened into, or frightened into, a promise made under duress is wrong and isn't valid, because a promise not freely made is not a promise, and a promise which is not a promise is not a true promise, and a promise which is not a true promise is a false promise, and a false promise is not worth anything, isn't a promise at all, and the two of us should have thought of that, Allan, but I'm not mad at you because of that, I should have said it right away, but it's only now that I can see it clearly, and I'm very happy about that, and since you helped me to see it I'm also thanking you . . ."

I had been talking to myself without looking at anything, maybe I had closed my eyes, but then I opened my eyes wide when I heard Mother's voice. She was standing in the doorway, staring at me in fright.

"You're delirious, child!" she shouted and ran over to tuck me back in under the comforter.

"No, Mother, I'm completely well, and I'd like to have dried cod!"

And then I explained the whole story to her.

At first she looked both astonished and angry, and three vertical creases formed between her eyes, but by and by the three stern furrows smoothed out and changed into smile wrinkles on each side of her eyes.

And when I finally stopped to ask whether she would forgive me for having tricked her, she laughed quietly:

"Yes, let's forget about it this time. But remember this for another time: there's something called paper and pencil!"

Now I wasn't one of those who claimed that grownups were always stupid and idiotic. Like Allan, for example, but he wasn't the only one. On the contrary, I thought my mother was smarter than most, even if she, like other grownups, I'll have to admit, could say or do something stupid now and then. And sometimes I myself got the idea that there were certain things in life which I understood better than my mother. Just as there were things which Allan had a more correct or personal understanding of than his mother or father. But I couldn't go along with branding all grownups dumb and idiotic. I thought many of them had their good reason for being and that in many cases it was to our advantage they were there. And vice versa. But now I realized more clearly than ever that they could have a head start on us simply by virtue of being older and having had more time to think things through a few times. If, that is, they had used time well. Like Mother, for instance. Now I could be upset that I myself hadn't thought of the idea of writing little secret notes to her. Especially since we had written so many secret notes to each other in school. And while I reveled in the all too salty dried cod I was already planning to write long letters to her after the time came for me to leave home. Something that deep down inside I hoped would never happen.

7

I didn't wait until three o'clock on Sunday to meet Allan. Usually when I have to do something embarrassing, such as to confess something, whether it is something I have done or not gotten done, I always manage to drag the time out, to remember seventeen very important things that have to be done first. For example, to visit an old aunt whom I otherwise never visit. 'That's exactly why it's important to visit her now!' I explain to my conscience, which always cheers me on in the direction of the more embarrassing alternative.

But this time there was nothing I needed to drag out. I have seldom been so eager to get something embarrassing over with. I rushed through breakfast, so when I got to Allan's house he wasn't finished with his oatflakes yet. We had the same favorite morning menu: a heaping serving of uncooked oatflakes in milk with sugar sprinkled on top, although there wasn't always much sugar in those days.

Allan's mother opened the door, now round and happy as usual:
"Good morning, Erling, tell me, did you fall out of bed or did you win in the lottery, you usually aren't up and around so early!"
"Good morning, Mrs. Nielsen, naw, I just wanted to visit you in this good weather!"
I spoke loudly so I could be sure Allan could hear me too. I enjoyed speaking loudly, I relished my own voice which could send attractive, well-shaped words out into the air as if that were the most natural thing in the world. Yes, I had fallen completely in love with my own voice. It was clear and cheerful but not exactly like a girl's voice, sharper than that, or angular, but not rough and cutting like Allan's or some of the others in our class whose voices were changing. It was clear, but manly, and I didn't tire of using it, so I continued:

"The sun is shining and the birds are singing, listen for yourself! A starling! It's shining, by the way. So you could always say: the birds are shining and the sun is singing!"

I stopped because I noticed I was about to become intoxicated by my own voice, and Allan's mother looked at me carefully, but then smiled: "You're really in high spirits—come on in and pass some of them on to him, my grouchy offspring!"

Allan sat bent over his mountain of oatflakes.

Each of us had his own way of eating oatflakes. I began at the top with the dry oatflakes, working my way steadily downward and ended up finally in the delicious mess on the bottom, where the oatflakes were swollen with sugary milk. That was the reward for eating my way through the dry part, or the dry part was the prelude to the real stuff.

But Allan began from the bottom, in the moat of milk around the castle of oatflakes. Not that he slurped up the milk first, rather he stuck his spoon in under the pile, dug tunnels so the milk could penetrate into the middle of the pile, which gradually collapsed. At a certain point, even though each of us began from a different direction, the landscapes of our oatflakes resembled the same marsh with its dry spots and wetlands, and probably tasted the same.

"Well, aren't you through with your grub yet?" I asked in a pushy loud voice, but he didn't look surprised.

"Be finished in a minute. You're up and about early."

I sat down and observed his plate. How come other people's sloppy oatflakes make an unappetizing impression, while your own oatflakes at the same stage turn your thoughts and tongue toward the Promised Land?

"What about the speaking strike?" I asked.

He glanced up with oatflakes in the corners of his mouth. I couldn't tell whether his surprised expression was genuine or put on.

"Well . . . you see . . ."

He lowered his eyes and spoon toward the sticky bog of oatflakes and kept on eating. In order to gain time, I could see that. The surprise was put on. He was so embarrassed that he completely forgot to ask why I had broken my part of the agreement.

I felt for him. But my inner voice, which was still stronger and manlier than my outer voice, said: "Hey, no pity. Get tough, otherwise you won't get to the bottom of the matter!"

So I waited. Finally he looked up again as he scraped together the last gluey bits with his spoon.

"You see, well, my old man came home yesterday, and you know..."

He probably expected that I was going to ask what happened, but I just looked at him. He repeated himself:

"And you know . . ."

My inner voice said: "No matter what I know or don't know, what it's all about is your idiotic idea about that speaking strike, so get to the point!" But I didn't let him hear my inner voice—not yet.

I looked at him without mercy as he sat there and squirmed. No, he wasn't squirming. He sat there stiffly and held his spoon in front of his face as if he intended to talk into it but couldn't find the button. Finally he said:

"Let's go down into the yard."

But at that instant his mother came in and announced:

"I'm going down now to hang some things out, and remember now, on Sundays you wash your own dishes—remind him of that, Erling."

As I have said earlier, Allan seldom said more than one sentence at a time. The speaking strike was the first thing that freed up his powers of oratory. His father had once compared him to a bottle of catsup you are trying to pound something out of: at first nothing comes, then still nothing comes, and then everything comes at once. That's the way it happened this time. As soon as his mother was down the stairs the words came rattling out of him faster than I could understand. But I will try to report the most important things.

For the rest of the afternoon Allan hadn't said a word to his mother, but then she hadn't spoken to him either, so she probably didn't catch on to the speaking strike.

At that time people worked on Saturdays too, but closed up at an earlier hour, so I don't know why his father came home later—he had probably been at the Ordrup Track to see a bicycle race. As soon as he came home, Allan's mother pressured him and seems to have suggested that he had to give Allan a swat or two. To this he answered something like:

"No, honeybunch, we should refrain as much as possible from hitting children. You can give little children a tap if they don't understand that they must not run in front of a streetcar. It's better to get a tap than get run over by Line 16, we're not going to disagree on that. But we must not hit big children who are almost adults, that won't do them any good, and I'll tell you why."

At this point I reminded Allan about the dishes so we went out into the kitchen, he washed and I dried while he continued his story.

His father had begun to tell about his childhood.

"When I was a kid, even until I was fifteen years old, my Dad would say to me: 'Go out in the yard and find a stick!' Then I knew for sure what was going to happen, because I was always doing something or other, that's the way I was, you know. So I went out and found a thin, little, rotten stick. Dad looked at it and said: 'Try to look around again, there must be a little better one.' So you see I had to go out again and find one that was a little thicker. But then he himself would go out and pull up a cabbage stalk, roots and all. It hurt, you can be darned sure, but that wasn't it. It was the cold calculating method. I would rather have had a solid thrashing right off the bat. Today Dad and I are great friends, but I still maintain it was wrong."

But then he began to ask Allan's mother just what had happened. Because he didn't think that someone would hit a person in the head with a cowboy magazine or anything else without having a reason. She must have said something or other to him.

She answered that she had quietly and calmly asked him to wash himself properly and to brush his teeth.

Then he said to Allan:

What's supposed to be so bad about washing yourself? Don't you realize that it's not a *duty* to wash yourself, it's a *right* all people have. Just imagine if I, with my job, didn't wash. Why, I'd be a disgrace! I wouldn't even go along with myself on the streetcar! Do you know what I would say to myself, I'd say, listen here, go home and wash up, you pig, you stink so badly that others can't draw a breath!"

Allan swore that he hadn't answered with a single word. He said his father had stared at him a little. Then he said to his mother:

"The boy is really in a huff. You must have said something or other to him." To which she answered: "Now you're starting up, too! I asked him to wash himself and brush his teeth."

"And then he threw *The Black Mask* right at your mask?"

"Go ahead and make fun of everything just like always!"

But Allan's father wasn't altogether satisfied with her account. He asked Allan again. Allan explained to me:

"Was I supposed to just sit there and put up with that? I shouted: 'She said my teeth were green!'"

He paused for a moment and listened whether anybody was on the stairway. Then he said: "That was it for the speaking strike. Well, sorry about that."

It was almost an historic moment. Allan wasn't one to go around apologizing. On the contrary, he always got us others to say we were sorry. Or in any case to feel that way toward him. Because he was always right. Even if you didn't always think he was right, he still proved himself right. Maybe because we were a little afraid of him, looked up to him too much. But perhaps more because, in a way, he *showed* himself to be right, even if he wasn't. Because he stood up for his ideas so stoutly, because he fought so fanatically for his ideas, we thought our own little right was downright little in comparison. Or you could say that we thought he *had the right* to be right whether it was wrong or not.

So when he now said to me he was sorry it was something totally strange. My bones became as soft as marzipan and my mouth watered. But I didn't want to give in now, either. I wanted to be tough. In addition I had to get tough with my inner voice, which had become completely meek and mumbled something about how after all I, too, had broken the speaking strike.

"That strike was not my idea, I explained all of that yesterday," I snarled back, "why not listen now and then?"

So my one inner voice was put in its place by my other inner voice. Now it was finally my outer voice's turn:

"What did they say to that?"

Allan looked at me in surprise. Already with some of that normal, overbearing, condescending, slightly impatient quality in his look. As if that was not something to be asked about. He said that of course his father just about died of laughter!

"Green teeth!" he said every time he caught his breath. "My big boy has green teeth! We can exhibit him for money, honeybunch, we'll be rich!"

Allan's mother still couldn't see anything funny in it.

"Just turn it into a joke like always!"

But he kept on:

"It's good enough for the Benneweis Circus, no, better yet, for Bakken Amusement Park and Kramer's Vaudeville[1]. The boy with the

---

[1] Some of Copenhagen's places for entertainment.

green teeth, step closer, ladies and gentlemen, one and all, tall and small, an extra event, we put some teeth into our show, as you can see—I'll lie on my back and read the Evening News all day—no, doggone it, I'll be his IMPRESSARIO, what do you say to that—what about you, oh, yes, you'll make sure his teeth stay green—every time you see a tooth brush in the vicinity you'll break it in two—we'll buy a house on Strandvejen[1], with parquet flooring in the ceiling—no, now I've got it: The Boy With the Emerald Teeth!—I've got to tell this to the boys tomorrow!"

"I dare you to!" Allan's mother said.

At this point in Allan's story we heard his mother coming up the stairs. Allan stuck his fingers in the corners of his mouth and pulled his lips away from his teeth.

They were white. Not chalky white, since almost no teeth are. But fairly white. Dazzling, I'll go that far. Then he let go of the corners of his mouth, and I couldn't read from his face whether he was completely serious when he said:

"To be on the safe side I first brushed them with soda. Then with powdered ammonia. And washed my mouth out with diluted hydrochloric acid. Three drops in half a cup of water. And finally once over with emery cloth."

"That's a lie!" I said.

"Do you think so?" he asked and tapped lightly on one of his shiny front teeth with the nail of his little finger. "In any case I'm not going to be exhibited for money!"

[1] Prestigious upper class section along Copenhagen's northern shore line.

SELECTED BIBLIOGRAPHY

Selected Bibliography

General:

Mitchell, P.M. *A History of Danish Literature.* 2nd augmented ed. New York: Kraus-Thomson, 1971. Contains valuable bibliographical information about Danish literature in English translation in addition to a comprehensive survey of Danish literature.

Anthology of Danish Literature, eds. Jansen, F.J. Billeskov and Mitchell, P.M. Carbondale: Southern Illinois University Press, 1971. A bilingual edition of representative examples from the Danish literature of the medieval period to the present; also available in a two volume paperback edition.

Contemporary Danish Poetry. An Anthology, eds. Line Jensen, Erik Vagn Jensen, Knud Mogensen, and Alexander D. Taylor. Copenhagen: Gyldendal and Boston: Twayne, 1977; contains also an introduction by the Danish critic Torben Brostrom which consists of a short characterization of modern Danish poetry.

The Devil's Instrument and other Danish Stories. Ed. by Sven Holm with an introduction by Elias Bredsdorff. London: Owen, 1971. Anthology of contemporary stories.

Modern Nordic Plays: Denmark. Ed. by E.J. Friis. New York: Twayne, 1974.

Works by Benny Andersen in English Translation:

Prism International, vol. 12, 1 (1973): "The Intellectual," trans. Hanne Gliese-Lee, p. 96 (poem).

Scandinavian Review, vol. 67, 2 (1979): "To a Strong Woman," trans. Nadia Christensen, p. 17; "Family Idyl," trans. Alexander Taylor, p. 16 (poems).

Selected Poems, trans. Alexander Taylor, Princeton: Princeton University Press, 1975; bilingual or English (paperback) only. A representative selection from Andersen's first seven volumes of poetry in excellent translations.

Seventeen Danish Poets, ed. Niels Ingwersen, Lincoln: Windflower Press, 1981, pp. 80-89: "To One Who Threw a Chair," "To SAS," "For Orientation," "Such a Morning," trans. Alexander Taylor. Bilingual.

The Devil's Instrument and other Danish Stories, ed. Sven Holm, London: Owen, 1971, pp. 247-60: "The Passage," trans. Paula Hostrup-Jessen (story).

The Evergreen Review, vol. 41 (1966): Tarzan. The Government. Refrigerators, trans. Ken Tindall, pp. 42-45; reprinted in *Evergreen Review Reader*, ed. Barney Rosset. New York: Grove Press, 1968, pp. 750-753 (story).

The Malahat Review, vol. 52 (1979): "The Drowning," trans. Elin Elgaard, pp. 28-40 (story).

Translation, Danish issue, vol. IX (fall 1982): "Compassion," "Heart in Snow," "Sponge Prince," trans. Alexander Taylor, pp. 3-5.

Benny Andersen: *Selected Stories:* Edited with an introduction to the author's works by Leonie Marx. Willimantic: Curbstone Press, 1982. 100 pp.

Works about Benny Andersen in English:

Marx, Leonie. "Benny Andersen." In *Encyclopedia of World Literature in the 20th Century.* 2nd revised and enlarged ed., vol. 1. New York: Ungar, 1981, pp. 83-84. General introduction to Andersen's works.

— . "Exercises in Living: Benny Andersen's Literary Perspectives," *World Literature Today,* vol. 52, 4 (1978), pp. 550-554. General presentation with specific analyses of a number of poems and the story "The Passage."

— . *Benny Andersen.* Twayne's World Author Series. Boston: G.K. Hall (forthcoming). A critical-analytical study of Andersen's work up to 1981.